Esther Charlotte Anne Allen

Echoes of heart whispers

Esther Charlotte Anne Allen

Echoes of heart whispers

ISBN/EAN: 9783744729277

Printed in Europe, USA, Canada, Australia, Japan

Cover: Foto ©Andreas Hilbeck / pixelio.de

More available books at **www.hansebooks.com**

ECHOES OF HEART WHISPERS.

BY

ESTHER CHARLOTTE ANNE ALLEN.

"Take thou these lays, they are
But sketches of a many-shaded mind,
Be the poor minstrel's memory there enshrined,
When she shall be afar."

MANCHESTER:
JOHN HEYWOOD, 141 AND 143 DEANSGATE,
LONDON: SIMPKIN, MARSHALL & CO.
1867.

TO

MRS FRANKLIN HOWORTH

This Volume

IS

MOST RESPECTFULLY AND AFFECTIONATELY

DEDICATED BY

THE AUTHORESS.

PREFACE TO THE FIRST EDITION.

IF any apology is due for presenting a new poetical effusion to the notice and reception of the public, it must be the desire to gratify the wishes of friends, who deemed it probable that others might find a few leisure hours enlivened by the simple Poems in which they have felt interested. If any sentiment therein contained should add the least influence to the side of Virtue, Temperance, and Piety, it will not be altogether in vain that these unpretending lays are launched on the sea of publicity.

43 UNION SQUARE, BURY,
July 21, 1866.

PREFACE TO THE SECOND EDITION.

WITH many thanks to the numerous friends who have so favourably received the first issue of her Work, the Authoress answers the demand for a Second Edition.

It has been carefully revised and corrected, and also considerably improved in appearance and size, containing a large number of additional Poems of recent date, which, with the original ones, she hopes will be found acceptable, and not unprofitable " Whispers" to many hearts in the few brief seasons of retirement amidst the hurry and bustle of life.

48 UNION SQUARE, BURY,
March 23, 1867.

CONTENTS.

HEART WHISPERS.

IN MEMORY OF A MOTHER.

 WILL not forget thee, mother ! when night'
    dark shadows flee ;
  In the hour of nature's freshness, mother
    I will think of thee ;
    For I miss thy gentle greeting, and the
      smile that lit thy face,
And earth may ne'er restore to me a mother's fond em-
  brace.

I will not forget thee, mother! when evening closes
  round,
When the queenly moon is sailing on, with starry diadem crowned ;
For perchance thy spirit may be near, a blessing to
  impart,
And to whisper in that holy hour sweet thoughts into
  my heart.

A

I will not forget thee, mother! in the hour of joy and
  mirth,
For thou lov'dst to see us happy whilst with us here on
  earth ;
I will strive to do and be, dear mother! what thou
  wouldst approve,
For dost thou not behold me with an angel's watchful
  love ?

And when clouds of sorrow cross my sky, then too I 'll
  think of thee,
And the Saviour that supported thee, shall then my
  refuge be ;
At morn—at even—in joy—in grief—thy memory still
  shall be
Cherished, my dearest mother! with earth's holiest love
  by me.

And when, by mercy guided through life's dangers, toils,
  and cares,
To my enraptured vision eternity appears,
Then shall I meet thee once again, and never more to
  part!
Till then thy memory shall be precious, mother! to my
  heart.

TO AN INFANT SLEEPING.

SLEEP on, sweet innocent! and fondly dream-
          ing,
     Of bliss it never may be thine to know,
  Enjoy the sunlight o'er thy visions stream-
          ing,
  Ere yet those visions bear a shade of woe.

Life's path to thee is strewn with flowers of gladness,
    Kind friends are round thee,—all is bright and fair;
A tender mother's love may chide the sadness,
    Or momentary shade thy brow may wear.

Each day unfolds some bright and new-found treasure
    Of beauty or of love to thy young heart;
A bird—a smile—a flower—an untold pleasure,
    To thy pure artless bosom may impart.

Alas! to think that innocence and brightness
    Like that which decks thine infancy must fade;
That thy young heart must lose its happy lightness,
    Thy brow be clouded by affliction's shade.

May He who watcheth o'er thy peaceful sleeping,
  Whose hand hath placed thee on life's changing road;
Still hold each change in providential keeping,
  To lead thee to His bright and blest abode!

Sleep on, sweet dreamer! and in peace reposing,
  Enjoy thy visions of earth's fancied bliss;
And when life's dreams, to thee for ever closing,
  Fade and recede;—be thine eternal happiness.

TO A DEPARTED SISTER.

Y sister! how that name is twined
    With all my fondest memories!
Thy look of love! thine accents kind!
    How have they waked my soul to
        bliss!

How would my childish bosom swell
    To hear thy lips some tale unfold,
That bound my heart with mighty spell,
    Though oft repeated—never old.

And when thou sang'st some plaintive strain,
    How has my heart rejoiced to hear!
Ah! never shall those strains again
    Thus charm my fondly listening ear.

I gazed, as closely to thy breast,
    With all a mother's holy love,
A beauteous cherub babe was prest,
    Bright as a sunbeam from above.

That cherub spread its hidden wing,
    And soared beyond our aching gaze ;
The accustomed song again to sing,
    In angel choirs—the song of praise.

The strains came floating to thine ear ;—
    Awake—asleep—by night—by day—
The spirit of thy darling near,
    Wooed thee to brighter scenes away.

And as earth's gently loosening ties
    (Not without many a pang) untwined,
Thy spirit joined her in the skies,
    And left our bleeding hearts behind.

Oh, when dark cares and sorrows press
    Around my path and cloud my sky,
'Tis then I feel my loneliness,
    And miss thy gentle sympathy.

Nor less when the deceiver, Hope,
    That lures too often to destroy,
With potent spell hath conjured up
    Some fairy dream of earthly joy.

Not less I miss thee then to share
    Its happiness, if such there be ;
Or with thy gentle hand to tear
    The illusive mask I cannot see.

Enough, fond heart! restrain thy grief!
　Whate'er thy Maker wills is best;
Fly to thy Saviour for relief—
　He'll soothe the anguish of thy breast.

Link not *her* memory with the dead—
　Mourn her not sleeping in the tomb;
Behold her risen with Christ, her Head,
　Encircled with unfading bloom.

STANZAS.

HOULD the tear of affection bedew
  The page that is now wet with mine,
When mouldering beneath the dark yew,
  Its branches shall o'er me entwine ;

May the heart that shall mourn my decease
  Ne'er taste of the pangs that rend mine ;
Ne'er wander a stranger to peace—
  Ne'er bend at Despair's gloomy shrine.

The world thinks me happy and gay,—
  I would not the world undeceive ;
Could its pity my cares drive away ?
  My heart's secret anguish relieve ?

Then why should I mourn or complain
  To those who no aid can impart ?
Whose kindliest efforts were vain
  To soothe the distress of my heart ?

In silence unpitied I sigh,
  And long for the hour of release ;
When the tear shall be wiped from my eye,
  And my soul gain the haven of peace.

ON FRIENDSHIP.

OH, breathe not thou lightly the name of a
    friend !
    Be it in tenderness spoken !
    Let not a cold slight the spirit bend,
    Nor affection's links be broken.
A harsh word—a careless look may wring
    With sorrow a trusting breast;
And a cloud o'er thy future pathway fling,
    An alloy o'er thy spirit's rest ;
Art thou pledged then to one, true, faithful, kind,
    At friendship's sacred shrine ?
Oh, cherish the holy links that bind
    That trusting heart to thine.

Perchance a cloud may shadow thy lot,
    And wring forth the bursting tears ;—
The bright hopes of youth be all forgot
    In the sorrows of coming years.
'Twill lighten thine heart of its load of care
    A faithful friend to find,
To bear in thy crushing griefs a share,
    And to calm thy troubled mind.

Art thou pledged then to one, true, faithful, kind,
 At friendship's sacred shrine?
Oh! break not the golden links that bind
 That trusting heart to thine.

'Twill sweeten thy cup of pleasure below,
 To share it with such a friend;
The hallowed joy 'twill be thine to know,
 Which sympathy only can lend.
And when earth's joys and troubles alike are o'er,
 True friendship a hope can give
The loved one to greet on a bright blest shore,
 And in friendship eternally live.
Art thou pledged then to one, true, faithful, kind,
 At friendship's holy shrine?
Oh! cherish the tie,—for death may but bind
 That heart closer—for ever—to thine.

THE TRIAL OF ABRAHAM.

THE morn arose in beauty and in light
　　O'er proud Moriah, towering o'er the plain.
　　'Twas now the third, since from his home
　　　　he came,
　　That aged patriarch : and the tear-drop
　　　　bright
Perchance fell gently from his dimming eye,
As he beheld the place where *he*, his Isaac, was to die.

But in submission to his Lord's command,
Nerved was his arm, and tutored was his will ;
Dark and mysterious though it seemed, yet still
He knew the event was in a Father's hand.
But oh ! with *him*, his promised one, to part !
Mighty—sublime—the faith that dwelt within that
　　parent's heart !

But yet a deeper chord within his breast
Was to vibrate : his inmost soul be stirred.
And oh ! when those long-cherished tones he heard,
" My Father ! " can his anguish be expressed

By insufficient words which mortals know ?
To think ere long *his* hand in death must lay the
    loved one low.

But faith hath stilled the tempest—on they pass—
At length the spot is gained—upraised the knife—
Against his promised heir—his Isaac's life—
Angels and fiends stand gazing witnesses ;
It is enough !   Oh, Abraham ! stay thy hand !
This bright example of thy faith throughout all time
    shall stand !

OLD AGE.

'TIS sweet in life's earliest morn when the
    heart
    Beats true to emotions of love and of
    truth ;
    And 'tis sweet, as the visions of childhood
    depart,
To feel the breast glow with the transports of youth.

What pleasure can equal the thrill of delight
    Aroused by the first tender whisperings of love ?
Oh ! what upon earth is so lovely and bright
    As the hopes and the joys that the young heart may
    prove ?

Ah ! deem not the picture thy fancy hath drawn
    Hath no dark shade to tinge its fair landscape with
    gloom ;
'Neath the roses of pleasure full many a thorn
    Lurks unseen till the short-lived flower ceases to
    bloom.

And hope, bland deceiver, too often betrays,
  And leaves the heart desolate, wretched, and lone ;
And the flower that blooms brightest too quickly de-
      cays,
  To call for a moment its beauty our own.

And frailties, and follies, and weaknesses crowd
  O'er the pathway of life, as we journey along ;
And affliction's bleak tempest, and sorrow's dark cloud,
  Blight the prospect where all breathed of beauty and
      song.

Bright and fair though life's morn be with sunshine
      and joy,
  Yet sweeter the calm and repose of its even ;
When wearied of hopes which a change may destroy,
  The spirit hath turned to its own native heaven.

True, the pleasures of youth have been proved to be
      vain,
  And fancy no longer rich colouring throws
O'er the trifles of earth ; but its grief and its pain,
  Temptations and sorrows, draw near to their close.

And oh ! to look back on life's path, and to trace
  Its mercies unnumbered, each day ever new,
Each snare and each danger, each time and each place,
  That the hand of a Father hath guided us through.

And to feel that the heart can repose in His love ;
  That He who hath kept will preserve to the end ;
This can yield consolation and peace far above
  The transient enjoyments a frail world can lend.

This can bring holy rapture and bliss to the heart,
  Unknown 'midst the ragings of passion and strife.
Then let youth with its fair fleeting visions depart,
  A brighter charm rests on the sunset of life.

WILD FLOWERS.

WILD flowers! wild flowers! beautiful are ye,
    Harbingers of summer hours! of joy, and
        song, and glee ;
    Roses proudly flinging on the air your
        fragrance sweet,
Modest violet springing from the moss beds at our feet.
Buttercups with golden heads, a countless multitude ;
Daisies in your humble beds, types of the meek and
    good ;
Lilies blooming modestly, sweet tenants of our vales ;
Blue bells whispering silently, of Scotia's hills and
    dales ;
Graceful cowslip, snowdrop fair, attendant on the
    spring ;
Various as the names ye bear, the memories that ye
    bring.
And thou, sweet unassuming flower, by love and friend-
    ship sought.
Entwining round affection's bower, lovely " Forget-me-
    not,"

Long years have swiftly sped along since first your
    charms I knew,
And yet I roam those charms among with pleasure ever
    new.
Though childhood's dreams have passed away, and left
    a void behind,
Yet ye are springing fresh and gay, as when with them
    ye twined ;
And when sad memory brings again the dreams of
    vanished joy,
A lingering look on you I cast, and check the rising
    sigh.

Wild flowers ! wild flowers ! warnings too ye give
Of the fleetness of the hours that I with you may live ;
Though now life's current tints my cheek, yet soon the
    time may come,
When I like you must droop and seek earth's dark and
    silent tomb.
Not only do ye link my heart to memories of the past,
But point to scenes of future bliss, which evermore
    shall last.
Proud, careless heart ! attend the voice, which from
    each floweret springs,
Oh ! fix not an immortal choice on transitory things ;
Emblems are we of all below, then raise thy hopes
    above,
Go to a changeless Saviour ! Go ! Repose in change-
    less love.

THE VOICE OF TEMPERANCE.

BRITAIN'S sons! securely dwelling
 In your land of matchless fame;
Ye whose patriot hearts are swelling
 At your much-loved Albion's name
As ye proudly read the story
Of your country's high renown,
Would ye that her wonted glory
 Still shall deck your England's crown!
Strive to save her! foes surround!
 Dangers threatening o'er her stand!
Strike Intemperance to the ground!
 Thus protect your much-loved land!

Britain's daughters! proud in beauty!
 Rich in loveliness and truth!
Yours is high and noble duty—
 To reclaim our sinking youth.
By your power to mould and fashion
 Hearts encaptived by your chain,—
By the all-prevailing passion,
 Your approving smile to gain,—

THE VOICE OF TEMPERANCE.

Bid them, ere they seek **your favour,**
  Nobly forth for Temperance stand,
Britain then shall hail **her** daughters
  Guardian angels of her land.

Britain's sires ! whose honoured memories
  Long shall live through future years ;
By the love ye bear your country,—
  By a parent's hopes and fears,—
Let not e'er the voice accusing
  Of your sons against you rise,
By thus thoughtlessly refusing
  Such a trivial sacrifice.
As ye wish your children happy,
  Oh ! no longer neutral stand !
Lead them in the paths of Temperance,
  Blessings to their native land !

Britain's mother ! fondly bending
  With affection deep, unknown,
O'er thine infant ; whilst ascending
  Speeds the prayer, " Lord, bless my son !"
Think what pangs of hopeless anguish
  Break full many a mother's rest,
As her hopes lie crushed and withered
  In the idol of her breast ;
Oh ! whilst yet his heart is tender,
  Join him to the Temperance band :
Thus shall champions rise around us
  Of the freedom of our land.

FORGET ME NOT.

FORGET me not, loved one,
 Though dark be my lot,
 Though friends have forsaken,
 And dear ones "are not."
 Yet, 'midst all earth's changes,
The thought of *thy* love
Would cheer my lone spirit,
 Like light from above.

But should e'er another,
 More lovely and true,
Possess that affection,
 That love *I* once knew ;
Or should I prove unworthy
 Of e'en thy regret,
Then cease to remember,
 Then thou mayst forget.

THE BROKEN-HEARTED.

HE hath passed away as some fair flower,
    That blossoms for a while,
Rejoicing 'neath the sunbeam's power,
    And gladdened by his smile.

But her sun hath set in starless night,
    And the flower hath ceased to bloom ;
She hath sunk 'neath a broken spirit's weight,
    To the dark and silent tomb.

She had treasured up in her gentle breast
    The brightest hopes of youth,
And had fondly deemed that earth possessed
    Hearts like her own for truth.

She trusted one,—and he cast away
    The love he had sought to gain ;
His was but the smile of an April day,
    As fickle, false, and vain.

But she murmured not, though her heart was sore,
That her youth's bright hope was fled,
Her cherished visions now no more ;
Joys—numbered with the dead.

The word of truth had marked a road,
And her footsteps gladly trod :
It led to the pure and bright abode
Of angels and of God.

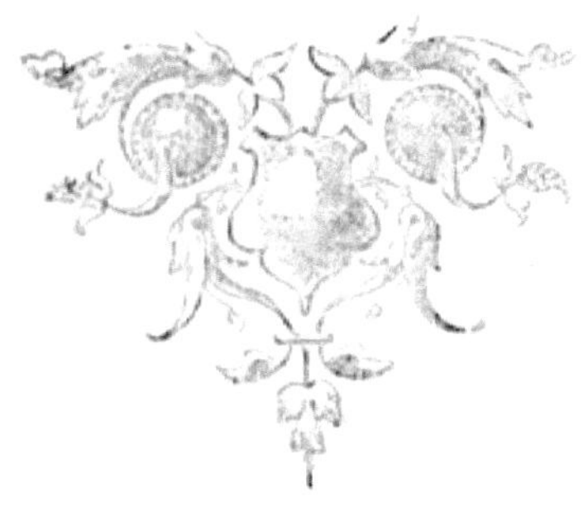

LINES TO A FRIEND.

WRITTEN AT THE AGE OF TEN YEARS.

FORGET me not, my dearest friend,
    When tossed on life's tempestuous sea ;
  Though troubles sore my path attend,
    Say, wilt *thou* still remember me ?
  Or, all unmindful of our early love,
Canst thou like the cold world forgetful prove ?

  No ! let me banish from my mind
    The thought that *thou* canst e'er deceive —
  The thought so cruel and unkind,
    That *thou* canst e'er forsake and leave
The friend with whom were passed such happy days
In innocent delight and childish plays.

TO MY MOTHER.

OTHER! farewell! thy transient race is run,
    Earth's trials o'er, its conflicts at an end,
Thy sun of life hath set whilst yet 'twas
      noon,
    And thou hast reached the goal to which
      we tend.

On thee fond memory dwells—for thee we weep,
    But soon we 'll greet thee on a brighter shore ;
" Death cannot wrap thee in eternal sleep,"
    And Heaven shall give thee to our arms once more.

TO THE SAME.

FAREWELL! but not for ever,
　　We soon shall meet again ;
Thou first hast crossed the river.
　　We shall not long remain.
Thy labours now are over,
Thou hast seized the blood-bought prize,
And thy memory shall be precious,
　　Till we meet thee in the skies.

THOUGHTS BY MOONLIGHT.

LOVE to gaze on the moonbeam fair,
When no sound disturbs the still, calm air;
When proudly sitteth the queen of night,
Robed in a mantle of silvery light,
And my thoughts have wandered fancy free,
In that hour of enchantment, to rest on
thee.
I think of thee—I think of thee—
As I gaze on the moonbeam fair,
I breathe for thee—I breathe for thee—
A fond and fervent prayer.

But 'tis not ever at day's decline,
The lovely planet deigns to shine;
Darkness may hold with iron chain
Undisputed her dreary and sombre reign.
So may the night of adversity shroud
And bury thy hopes 'neath sorrow's cloud.
But I 'll think of thee—I 'll think of thee—
When the moonbeam's past away;
Still true to thee—still true to thee—
My love be thy guiding ray.

TO AN EARLY FRIEND.

FRIENDS may part, and distance sever
   Hearts that beat with friendship true ;
But not friends nor distance ever,
   Can that friendship's warmth subdue.

Though in far-off climes they wander,
   Though the deep betwixt them roll,
" Absence makes the heart grow fonder,"
   Friendship firm unites each soul.

'Tis a pure and tender passion,
   Planted deep within the heart ;
Granting hope and consolation
   Under every trying smart.

Such the friendship that I bear thee,
   Such the love that fills my breast,
Time or absence cannot tear thee
   From the heart so long possest.

Fare thee well ! 'midst all earth's changes,
   Faithful still I 'll think of thee,
And whene'er thy memory ranges
   O'er the past, remember me !

ON IMMORTALITY.

CHILD! rejoice!   To thee is given
     Being that shall never end ;
    Joys of earth, and hopes of heaven,
     On thy pathway to attend.
     Life hath opened bright on thee,
   Life which nought can e'er destroy ;
Noble is thy destiny,
   Thou shalt never—never die.

Youth! rejoice!   'Tis thine to know
   Purest bliss that mortals prove,
Chain not thy desires below,
   Raise thy heart and hopes above.
Forward! press to yon bright goal,
   Let not earth thy steps arrest ;
'Tis beneath the immortal soul,
   On its transient bliss to rest.

Man! rejoice!   Though now no more
   Youth's bright hopes and joys are thine ;
Soon thy conflicts shall be o'er,
   Thine be pleasures pure, divine.

Rest not! pause not! look not back
    On the days for ever flown!
Onward! on the shining track
    Leading to the eternal throne.

Sinner! weep!   True, life is thine,
    Youth's bright hopes, or manhood's cares;
But upon that life's decline
    Hangs a cloud of gathering fears.
Haste thee! ere the whirlwind come!
    Rouse thee! ere thou sleep in death!
Seek beyond the skies a home;
    Seize it thine through conquering faith.

L O V E.

OVE! noblest of the various passions that animate the human breast! Source of the most ecstatic pleasure, of the most refined delight! Whether we view thee as the connecting link of hearts formed for each other, sweetening the joys, and alleviating the sorrows of life; forming an adamantine chain that nought but death can sever;—or see thee beaming from the eye of a mother resting on the sweet prattler at her side;—or the lovely infant pressed to her bosom;—or contemplate thee as the ruling principle in the breast of an affectionate child, gently soothing and comforting the declining years of a revered and beloved parent; or follow thee to the haunts of grief and wretchedness, and behold thee pouring the balm of consolation into the wounds of affliction or distress. In whatever light we view thee, lovely is the aspect thou wearest. 'Tis thine to scatter flowers of gladness over the dreary pathway of life. How wretched must the heart be that hath nought to call forth the noblest attribute of its nature—that hath nought to love! How dark the

horizon uncheered by thine heavenly ray. And yet
" our life may not be all a dream of love, else were
this cold and barren earth too blest." No. Thy mission is not by rendering earth more delightful, to reconcile our hearts to it as our resting-place. Our
natures are too degenerate to enjoy Heaven's blessings
in perfection whilst here below. It is not even in *thy*
power, all-conquering though it be, to produce pleasure
unalloyed by pain. The thought, that the most beloved of earth will ere long as the dew, or the clouds,
pass from our sight, will too often intrude on our happiest moments, and cast a shade of anguish over the
sunshine thou hast brought. But we do not see thee
in thy beauty ; we do not contemplate thee in thy true
character, as relating only to earth. Mark yon humble
Christian ! His actions, his walk, his converse. How
carefully he shuns sin ! How nobly he stands where
thousands fall ! As he wends his way along his pilgrimage, he leaves a shining track behind him of bright
and noble deeds ; of suffering alleviated, — sorrows
soothed—hearts consoled. " Freely ye have received,
freely give," is the precept to which he lends a prompt
and willing obedience. Whence comes his fear of of-
fending God ? whence his patient kindness to his enemies, to those who persecute and wrong him ? Whence
his anxiety for the happiness of all around him ? All
spring from one source, deep, mighty, inexhaustible ;
'tis Love, pure, heaven-born Love, that actuates his
breast, subduing every earthly and baser feeling, ennobling and elevating his mind above the ever vacillat-
ing motives and impulses of a changing world. It is

this heavenly principle that rules within his breast; purifying it from earthly dross, raising his whole soul into communion with its own mighty source; till at length, fully transformed and renewed, the heaven-born spirit shall be exhaled from its clayey tabernacle, and bathe in the full ocean of immortal delight and blessedness; for ever lost in God, for God is Love.

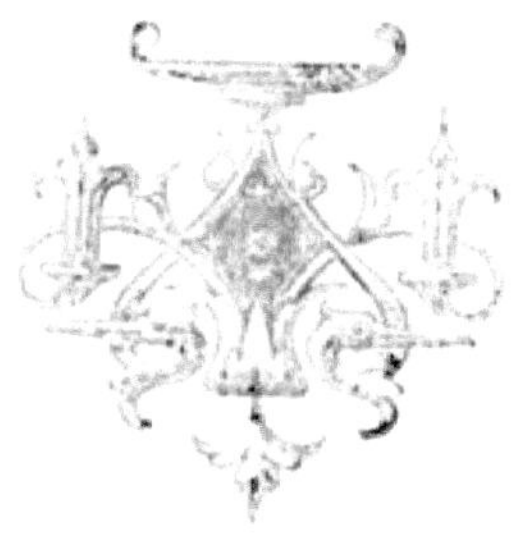

ON VISITING A SUPPOSED HERMITAGE

NEAR BAKEWELL, DERBYSHIRE.

THY lot be mine ! a peaceful, calm retreat,
    Far from the busy changing scenes of life,
    The city's clamour, and the hamlet's strife ;
        A lone sequestered spot,
        By all the world forgot,
Hallowed by prayer and contemplation sweet.

Thy envied lot be mine ; thus to resign
Pleasures of earth, deceitful vanities,
To drink the ever-flowing streams of bliss
        Which those alone can know.
        The happy chosen few,
Whose lives shall pass pure, undefiled as thine.

But hark ! what softly strikes my listening ear ?
From yonder village floats the song of praise,
Mellowed by distance ; and the harmonious lays
        Check fancy, and suggest
        The query to my breast,
Couldst thou indeed find purest pleasures here ?

C

Ah! were it noble thus to quit the field ?
Not so thy Saviour taught.   He bade to be
As salt,—light,—cities,—that the world might see,
    And seeing might adore
    And magnify His power,
Who is our glorious Captain, Sun, and Shield.

The spell is broken which had conjured up
A superstitious reverence for the man,
Whose days in idle, useless tenour ran.
    Be mine a nobler part,
    To tread with fearless heart
The path of duty cheered by faith and hope.

THE YOUTHFUL POETESS.

SHE sat by the taper's lessening light,
    But she heeded not its decline;
    For the book had dropped from her nerve
        less hand,
    And her spirit had sought an enchanted land
And had bent at fair Poesy's shrine.

She had read the burning words of one
    Who had wandered earth's beauties among;
Whose heart had glowed with a holy fire
Which had guided the pen, and attuned the lyre
    To high and lofty song.

And she, too, the inspiration caught,
    As she mused o'er the raptured strain;
That night, ere sweet slumber had soothed her breast,
Her prayer had been uttered—her wild wish exprest,
    To live, but the like fame to gain.

Her prayer was answered, her heart attuned
    To wild and beautiful lays.
From her pen dropped gems of noble thought,
And she found what her heart so eagerly sought—
    The meed of earthly praise.

Proudly she pressed on her bright career,
   Upheld by the breath of fame,
But little they deemed who the tribute paid
That her youth's first holiest powers were laid
   On the shrine of an earthly name.

But the spoiler came, and quenched the light
   That dwelt in her beaming eye.
He withered the rose on her youthful cheek,
And bid her, her lonely chamber seek,
   And she knew that she must die.

And oh, what anguish filled her breast
   As she thought on her misspent hours !
On the blessings she ne'er had sought to prove—
On a Saviour's slighted, neglected love—
   On the waste of her youthful powers.

Oh, where was the praise she had loved to hear ?
   'Twas now but an empty breath.
No aid, alas ! could its voice impart
To soften her sorrow or cheer her heart,
   Bowed down by the hand of death.

Lowly and humbled she sought her part
   In her Saviour's slighted love ;
Her spirit turned from earth's trifles away,
And her heart was attuned to a sweeter lay,
   As she joined the redeemed above.

FAREWELL TO ALBION.

FAREWELL, my native land!   Blest Albion's
      happy strand,
    Scene of my earliest years, Youth's hopes
      and Manhood's cares,
      I leave thee with an aching heart ;
For oh, 'tis hard with ties as strong as thine to part !

Fond Memory travels back along my life's short track,
The scenes to Childhood dear, touched by her wand
      appear
    In brighter, fairer colours seen ;
Through the long shading years that darkly roll be-
      tween.

And now I leave behind my native land, to find
Perchance a brighter sky and flowers of sweeter dye,
    But still my heart shall linger here,
And thoughts of home awake a tributary tear.

O Thou who rul'st on high, Sov'reign of earth and sky,
Whose power is infinite !   Now from Thy mercy-seat
    Infuse Thy love into my breast,
And guide my wand'ring feet to their eternal rest.

THE ANGELS' SONG.

Glory to God in the highest, on earth peace, good-will towards men."

WEETEST of sounds e'er repeated by man!
　Sweetest of songs e'er by seraphim sung;
When shall the wide world re-echo the strain
　Which once in its sweetness o'er Bethle-
　　hem rung?

There was the glorious banner unfurled,
　Bidding earth's tumults and discords to cease;
Gladly a weary and battle-worn world
　Started to gaze on the ensign of peace.

Immanuel Himself sealed its motto with blood,
　And the cross in its heavenly texture was wrought,
And spreading its triumphs o'er field and o'er flood
　It hath waved, whilst glad millions its shadow have
　　sought.

And still shall it triumph, till heart after heart
　Shall joyfully catch and re-echo the strain—
Till all in the universe chorus take part
　Of " Glory to God and good-will unto men."

LINES ACCOMPANYING A BIBLE AS A BRIDAL GIFT.

NOT costly gems I offer thee on this thy bridal
    day,
    For were they mine to give, love, their
        brightness must decay ;
    The pearl of price alone, love, a fadeless
        light shall shed ;
May its blest precepts guide thy life, its blessings crown
    thy head.
To wish thee cloudless skies, love, and calm unruffled
    seas,
Might well express my fond desires; but ah, earth
    yields not these !
I wish thee what thou mayst enjoy, God's smile and
    heavenly peace,
And when earth's dearest pleasures fly, eternal happi-
    ness.

MEMORY.

H, say not memory is a friend
　　To hearts oppressed with grief,
　That thoughts of bygone joys can lend
　　The troubled soul relief.

When crushed beneath a weight of cares,
　What recks it then to dwell
On the lost peace of other years,
　Remembered but too well?

When keen misfortune's withering blast
　Hath nipped hope's tender bloom,
Ah, what avails its beauty past
　To raise it from the tomb?

One friend remains, but 'tis not this,
　For memory must confess,
No power hath she to waken bliss
　'Midst clouds of dark distress.

'Tis love almighty, sovereign love!
　This power, and this alone,
Shall light the darkness with a ray
　From the celestial throne.

WELCOME TO SPRING.

BEAUTIFUL Spring! enrobed in smiles,
Thy loveliness e'en dull care beguiles.
Thou com'st with the voice of the wild
bird's note,—
With the sweet sounds that o'er the wood-
land float ;
Thou com'st in a vest of thousand dyes,
And perfumes rich from thy footsteps rise.
" The air is balm," and the soul drinks in
A breath wafted from heaven to a world of sin.
A voice from the skies thou echoest along
In whispers of beauty, of hope, and of song.
What though we muse on the friends that are gone ?
They shall rise as the grain that in hope hath been sown.
What though we mourn for the joys that are fled ?
Others shall spring to our hearts in their stead.
What though this earth hath nought more to bestow,
And every enjoyment seems withered below ?
Spring shall arise, an eternal spring,
And crown us with flowers unwithering.

What though in poverty doomed to sigh?
Let us chase the faithless tear from the eye;
Whilst birds and flowers ask with voices of joy,
Will *our* watchful Protector leave *thee* to die?
Beautiful Spring! we welcome thee!
Dear to our hearts may thy teachings be!

THE THREE WELCOMES TO CHRISTMAS.

WELCOME! welcome! merry Christmas,
　　With the gladness that thou flingest.
Welcome! welcome! merry Christmas,
　　With the good things that thou bring-
　　　est.
Holidays and happy faces,
　　Plum-puddings and mince-pies;
Mirth and song and merry pastime,
　　And loving, laughing eyes.

I love thee, merry Christmas,
　　For the sweet and pleasant story,
Of the manger-cradled baby,
　　The Lord of life and glory;
Of the angels and the shepherds,
　　And the star so bright and mild.
Welcome! welcome! merry Christmas
　　To the bosom of a child.

MANHOOD'S WELCOME.

I welcome thee, Old Christmas, but not with heart as
    light
As I was wont to greet thee on this glad and festive
    night :
For my spirit hath been wand'ring in life's bewild'ring
    maze,
To realise my childhood's dreams, those dreams of
    happier days.
And as I muse on buried hopes, and friends, like them,
    departed,
Oh ! blame me not, if from my eye the tear of sorrow
    started.
        But I would not check
        The hopes that deck
     Childhood's bright hours of gladness,
        But catch a ray
        To chase away
     My gloom and pensive sadness.
Then a welcome still, Old Christmas ! a welcome full
    and free !
Cold indeed must be the bosom that cannot welcome
    thee.

OLD AGE'S WELCOME.

    Welcome ! old friend, once more,
      Many times we thus have met ;
    And thou comest once again
      And find'st me lingering yet.

In childhood's happy moments
  I 've rejoiced thy face to see ;
And in manhood's whirl of busy care
  I still have welcomed thee :

In joy, and song, and gladness,
  With loved friends to share a part—
In sorrow and in sadness,
  And loneliness of heart.

Fond memory calls up scene by scene,
  Where year by year we 've met,
And friends that one by one have been
  Cut down, and I 'm here yet.

But the tale that charmed my infancy,
  Of the illustrious birth
Of the wondrous Babe of Bethlehem,
  By angels sung on earth,

Hath now a deeper power to charm
  My heart as well as ear ;
For I 've proved its wondrous potency
  Through many a changing year.

It hath checked my boyhood's wildness ;
  It hath borne through manhood's cares ;
It hath shed a holy calmness
  O'er life's declining years.

I love thee still, old Christmas!
   And to see youth welcome thee,
And I feel myself a child again
   As their noisy mirth I see.

Twined with dearest recollections
   Com'st thou again to me,
Then hail! old happy Christmas,
   I gladly welcome thee.

"ARE THEY NOT ALL MINISTERING SPIRITS?"

HOW sweet the thought that when we wake or
    sleep,
  Or toil, or rest—some angel form is near,
O'er us celestial watch and guard to keep,
  Our lagging, fainting, heavenward steps
    to cheer!

In danger's hour to encamp, (no transient guest,)
  And ward away each secret, deadly blow,
Aimed with undying malice at the breast,
  By our unseen, but mighty spirit-foe.

To breathe a heavenly influence o'er the soul,
  Allied by faith to omnipresent love ;
To teach that faith to pierce these mists that roll
  So darkly round ; and gaze on things above.

Thus good Elisha sat, unmoved with dread,
  Though Syrian warriors encamped around ;
Though near they came, the prophet's blood to shed,
  Nearer he saw celestial hosts surround.

And thus was Daniel, in the trying hour,
  Defended by a form of heavenly light ;
An angel's hand restrained the lion's power,
  An angel's presence cheered the gloomy night.

Thus prisoned Peter, sleeping in his cell,
  Was startled by a messenger from heaven,
Whilst from his hands the iron fetters fell,
  And wonderful deliverance was given.

Thus Paul, in shipwreck's wild and fearful hour,
  Was kept in sweet tranquillity and peace ;
For one bright form had spoken words of power,
  To still his fears and bid his doubtings cease.

Let those reject the sweet and soothing thought,
  Who take no evidence they cannot see ;
Where inspiration's page the truth has taught,
  The view it gives is full of joy to me.

Are they not ministering spirits ? sent
  To minister unto the heirs of heaven ?
Rejoice they not when contrite hearts repent,
  And to the penitent sweet peace is given ?

I heard a tale—an artless, simple tale,
  And told in all the confidence of truth ;
Ripe years lent weight to every word that fell,
  It was no idle phantasy of youth.

The summer skies smiled in unclouded light
    Upon a wayside cottage in a lane ;
Whose door led out into a garden bright,
    Where flowers sent answering smiles to heaven again.

But in that cot, with sorrow-stricken breast,
    Sat one—from whose dark life all hope seemed fled ;
Despair with gloomy hand her bosom prest,
    With anguish throbbed her weary, aching head.

Dark thoughts—alas ! *how* dark what pen shall say ?—
    Come gloomily and strangely o'er her brain.
" Oh ! should her trembling hand at once essay
    To rid herself alike of life and pain ?"

A sudden startle drives these thoughts away,—
    A knock—an entrance at th' half-opened door,—
A comely stranger speaks—" Come ! let us pray,"
    And reverently he kneels upon the floor.

She kneels—and holy influences rest
    And brood around them as they lowly bend,
And lo ! each secret feeling of her breast,
    Stands forth revealed by this mysterious friend.

A more than mortal unction fires his tongue,
    As all her wants before her God he lays ;
Griefs hid within her heart too deep—too long—
    She hears and feels are open to his gaze.

He prays, (and oh ! the fervour of that prayer !)
  That God may keep her in " th' unequal strife,"
May give her strength her heavy cross to bear,
  Or chase away the clouds that darken life.

She felt his prayer was answered.   As he spoke,
  The heavy weight of sorrow rolled away ;
Celestial sunlight o'er her spirit broke,
  And kindled up anew hope's flickering ray.

He rose,—he crossed the threshold, and no more
  Was seen by her astonished, wondering eye :
Awestruck, she stood within the opened door,—
  To right—to left—no trace could she espy.

The garden path led from the public road—
  Unseen by her he could not pass away ;
No evening's deepening gloom his form might shroud,
  The pathway lay beneath the eye of day.

Nor greeting, nor farewell he breathed to her.
  " Come ! let us pray !" he said, and bowed the knee ;
But on her inmost heart was stamped that prayer,
  So full of holy power and majesty.

At the same hour, within a house remote,
  Her husband sat, with vain companions round
A nameless, sudden fear his conscience smote,—
  A mighty influence his spirit bound.

The glass just lifted to his longing lip,
  Was suddenly arrested in his hand;
He tried again,—in vain,—he could not sip,
  Some inward power asserted strange command.

He rose,—he left the house, and sought his home,
  To hear his wife the wondrous fact declare,
How a mysterious visitant had come
  And offered up a spirit-searching prayer.

And he too told how, by a hidden power,
  His heart and hand were checked in sin's career;
And now, within that sacred, solemn hour
  They mingled prayer with prayer, and tear with tear.

Her troubled heart at length had found its rest,
  Their prayers were heard and answered from above
The dove of peace again upon each breast
  Brooded, and shed sweet calm and heavenly love.

For many years their footsteps jointly trod
  Life's pilgrimage, cheered by their Saviour's smile.
The old man now is gone to be with God,
  But Mary lingers here a little while.

And though proud scepticism may turn away,
  And though philosophy, with reason's power,
May strive the supernatural to gainsay—
  She still the tale unfolds of that mysterious hour.

TO CONSUMPTION.

AH ! fell Consumption ! with thy deadly power
  And stealthy footstep,—stealing unaware,
E'en to the heart's core of the fairest flower,
  And fixing thine envenomed arrow there.
    Not tears of pity—not impassioned sighs—
Nor torturing fears that rack the lover's breast ;
Nor parent's fondest prayer—nought may suffice
  To tear from thee thy prey, or thy relentless hand
    arrest.

And thou dost mark the loveliest for the tomb,
  The brightest—fairest—whose brief span of time
Hath ripened into more than mortal bloom,
  The blossoms destined for a deathless clime.
The gentlest spirits that have cheered our hearts
  Like gleams of sunshine in life's cloudy day,
But oh ! the pang, as one by one departs,
  And the too loved ones pass from our too fond
    embrace away.

But we will murmur not, though cold thine hand
    Falls on our brightest prospects—withers up
The few exotics of our desert land
    That tempt our stay ; and cuts off every hope
That centres in terrestrial objects.   Still
    Unerring love and wisdom we adore,
And bow submissive to our Maker's will,
    Till summoned to that land where thou shalt cloud
        our bliss no more.

THE SISTER'S WISH TO AN ABSENT BROTHER.

THOU art gone from our side, and we may
    not behold thee;
    Between us the waves of the ocean lie
      spread;
    But oh! may the arms of thy Saviour
      enfold thee,
And Heaven's choicest blessings descend on thine
    head.

We have known thee, and loved thee, ere moments of
    sorrow
    Had darkened the sunshine that dwelt on thy brow;
When thy heart was unburdened with cares for the
    morrow,
    And hope's richest beams cheered thy pathway below.

And shall we then love thee less fondly—sincerely,—
    Now the world hath forsaken and left thee alone?
Ah, no! our fond hearts may but prize thee more dearly,
    Now the dreams that beguiled thee for ever are flown.

May the Saviour protect thee—assist thee—defend
        thee—
    His love be thy portion—His Word thy delight—
May that blessing which addeth no sorrow attend thee,
    Through this dark vale of tears, to the mansions of
        light.

And though thou art gone, and we may not behold thee,
    And between us the dark ocean waters lie spread ;
Yet, oh ! may the arm of thy Saviour enfold thee,
    And Heaven's choicest blessings be showered on thine
        head.

"THEN HE AROSE AND REBUKED THE WIND AND THE WAVES, AND THERE WAS A GREAT CALM."

HARK! to the midnight tempest's sullen roar!
See! the wild billows furious lash the shore!
The angry winds, with fierce, resistless sweep,
Stir up the mighty bosom of the deep.
See! yon frail vessel, tossed upon the wave!
Yon seamen, shrinking from a watery grave!
Fear fills each breast and trembles in each eye;
Despairing they survey the danger nigh.
But One there is, unmoved by dread alarm,
Securely sleeps, nor heeds impending harm;
Peace o'er His couch her downy pinions spreads,
And quiet slumber o'er tired nature sheds.
His loved disciples round Him trembling stand,
And gaze with wistful eyes towards the land.
Reposing there, they see their Master lie,
Then wake Him with a supplicating cry—
Oh! save us! Jesus! by thy mighty power!
Save! or we perish, in this dreadful hour!

Just such their fear as that the sinner feels,
When the keen sense of guilt and danger steals
Into his heart, o'erwhelmed with sinking dread,
And vengeance hangs o'er his devoted head.
No human power can bid the tempest cease,
Or fill the wearied, sin-tossed soul with peace.
But mark the Saviour! with a tender look,
But chiding voice, their faithless fears rebuke :
Ah! wherefore did ye doubt ! Ah! tremblers! why
Thus in effect my power and love deny?
Majestic He arose, and stretched His hand—
The winds and waves obey His high command.
Their raging ceases at their Maker's nod,
And earth and air confess the Incarnate God :—
Hushed to a calm their mighty tempests cease,
And all is quietness, repose, and peace.

EARTH AND HEAVEN.

CHILD of frail mortality!
   Weep! for though this earth is fair,
All its brightness shall decay—
   Pleasures vanish into air.
  All that most thine heart doth prize,
Soon shall lose its transient worth;
Each revolving moment cries—
   Fleeting are the joys of earth.

Child of immortality,
   Though this earth is fleet as fair,
All thy hopes may rest on high—
   Heavenly pleasures wait thee there.
Though earth's brightest joys decay,
   Brighter far to thee are given:
Let its transports die away—
   Lasting is the bliss of heaven.

IS A DRUNKARD A MAN?

LINES SUGGESTED BY AN ORATION DELIVERED BY

J. B. GOUGH.

WHAT! and is *this* a man? with godlike soul
   And faculties for noblest ends designed;
With feelings,—thoughts,—desires beyond
    control,
   Ranging through space unfathomed, un-
    confined?

Is *this* a man? with power to stand and gaze
   Into yon heavens, and read creative skill;
A being formed to love, and pray, and praise,
   To learn and do his bounteous Maker's will?

Is *this* a man? upon whose infant face
   Were pictured beauty, innocence, and joy;
Once folded in a mother's fond embrace,
   Whose heart-strings twined around her darling boy?

Is *this* a man? who owns the sacred name
  Of husband! father! all that heart holds dear—
Whose breast can feel a sympathetic flame,
  A love impassioned, tender, deep, sincere?

Is *this* a man? for whom the Saviour bled—
  For whom the King of glory stooped beneath—
For whom a painful, suffering life He led,
  For whom endured an agonising death?

Yes! Christian!   'Tis a man! one such as thou,
  With hopes, desires, aspirings, such as thine;
Though dark, degraded, miserable now,
  A blinded votary at a demon's shrine.

Yes! 'tis a man!   The same creative power
  That bade thee be,—breathed forth his spirit too;
A man—that must exist when Time 's no more:
  An heir of endless happiness or woe.

Yes! 'tis a man! upon whose infant face
  Hath rested an enraptured mother's eye;
Delighted in each feature there to trace
  The promise-marks of future pride and joy.

Yes! 'tis a man! a husband, father, friend,
  For whom the tear-drop of affection rolls;
Upon whose influence and example 'pend
  The destinies of never-dying souls.

Yes ! 'tis a man !   For him the Saviour died,
   His soul was ransomed, but with blood divine ;
For him in agony the Sufferer cried,
   Father ! I shrink ! yet not *My* will, but Thine !

And, Christian ! canst thou read the high command—
   That, as thyself, thy neighbour shall be dear,—
And, longer wavering, hesitating stand,
   And see thy wretched brother weltering there ?

Nay ! let not pride within thy bosom rise,
   Nor strive to save with cold and haughty look :
Against thee all his native pride shall rise ;
   Such treatment thy own spirit ill could brook.

Stoop, humbly stoop ! his wanderings to reclaim ;
   Lower for thee, thy Saviour stooped to atone :
Vow to detest the cause that caused his shame,
   That its unhallowed spell hath o'er him thrown.

And though by virtue of restraining grace
   Not for thyself the abstemious vow be made ;
Yet, should that ransomed sinner find a place
   Amongst the blest, shalt thou not be repaid ?

"MY PEACE I GIVE UNTO YOU."

EACE to the troubled soul,
    With conscious guilt oppressed ;
One look at Calvary—
One prayer-fraught, faith-winged sigh,
    And the burdened soul hath rest—
        There is peace.

Peace to the tempest-tossed,
    By waves of sorrow driven ;
Though high the billows roll,
They cannot drown the soul ;
    For the anchor enters heaven—
        There is peace.

Peace ! when earth's fondest ties
    By one sad stroke are riven ;
Sorrowing, not without hope,
The tear-filled eye looks up
    To a meeting-place in heaven—
        There is peace !

"MY PEACE I GIVE UNTO YOU."

Peace ! to the stricken one,
   Weeping the silent dead ;
One Friend remains above,
And the heart rests in His love ;
   Though earthly hopes are fled,
      There is peace !

Peace ! in the last dread hour
   Ending life's fitful dreams ;
Scattering the deepening gloom,
Illumining the tomb,
   Immortal radiance streams—
      All is peace !

I WOULD NOT BE FORGOT.

 WOULD not be remembered, love,
    When thy heart is full of glee ;
  I would not have thy mirthful hours
    Disturbed by thoughts of me.
    But when thy joyous gladness, love,
  Shall yield to sober thought ;
In thy hours of pensive sadness, love,
  I would not be forgot.

I would not be remembered, love,
  When proudly thou shalt rise ;
When the praise and fame of thousands, love,
  Exalt thee to the skies.
But, oh ! should dark adversity
  With thorns o'erspread thy lot,
Then, in that hour of anguish, love,
  I would not be forgot.

I would not be remembered, love,
  When friends around thee throng,
When proudly thou shalt tread, love,
  The halls of mirth and song.

But, oh! should friends forsake thee,
   And shun thy altered lot,
Then, in that hour of loneliness,
   I would not be forgot.

I would not be remembered, love,
   When in the cold tomb laid;
I would not o'er thy youthful mind
   My memory cast a shade.
But when long years have sped away,
   And thou, in pensive thought,
Shalt number o'er sincerest friends,
   I would not be forgot.

A VALENTINE.

THOU camest like a vision bright
    Across my life's dark sky,
  With thy brow of inspiration,
    And thy deep, expressive eye ;
    Thy rich melodious voice, which woke
  Its echoes in my heart ;—
But I knew not that I loved thee,
  Till I knew that we must part.

On such a form as thine, in dreams,
  Enraptured I have gazed ;
And worshipped, in my waking hours,
  The idol fancy raised.
It was not beauty, honours, wealth,
  Around that idol twined,
That won my heart's first, purest love—
  'Twas nobleness of mind.

A heart that fondly owned the sway
  Of music's witching power,
Nor deemed it folly to devote
  A thoughtful, passing hour,

To roam through those Elysian fields,
  Where many a floweret blooms,
Of which proud Albion twines her wreaths
  To deck her poets' tombs.

All this, and more, I found in thee,
  And fancy was at rest ;
A form had shrined the fondly-worshipped
  Idol of my breast.
And as I gazed upon *thy* brow,
  And listened to *thy* voice,
I yielded to a secret spell,
  That bade my heart rejoice.

Forgive the wish that prompted me
  My love thus to avow ;
Thou mayst not see the burning blush
  That crimsons o'er my brow ;
Suffice it that thou know'st one heart
  Is changelessly thine own—
One that can brave the storms of fate,
  And dare to love alone.

I mourn not that we thus have met ;
  'Tis well that love like mine
Were raised from transitory bliss,
  And fixed on hopes divine.
And oh ! amongst those hopes, shall one
  Have power to cheer my breast,
To meet thee in a happier land—
  The regions of the blessed.

Farewell ! and through each scene of life,
    Its changing hopes and fears,
The clouds or sunshine that shall deck
    Or darken future years,
May the prayer affection breathes for thee
    Be o'er thee as a spell ;
And blessings be around thy path :
    Belovèd, fare-thee-well !

TO A YOUNG LADY IN DECLINE.

FAIR flower! thus sweetly blown—thus early
      smitten,
    In all thy youthful loveliness and bloom;
  Sinking, by pale disease, thy verdure bitten,
    Consumption's victim, to an early tomb.

Shall we repine that He who brought thee hither,
    And bade thee grace a while our garden bower,
  Saw fit so soon thine opening charms to wither,
    And gather to Himself the fragrant flower?

No! though a thousand tender ties are twining
    Our hearts to thine, so gentle and so good,
  We will not, by a sinful, vain repining,
    Arraign the love or wisdom of our God.

Go! for this earth may not detain thy spirit,
    By aught that it can offer.   Brighter far
  The glories thou art hastening to inherit:
    Go! may we act thy wish, and live to meet thee
        there.

LINES WRITTEN IN A CHURCHYARD.

WEETLY and peacefully rest the dead,
  In their long home—their narrow bed;
  They have fought their fight, they have run
    their race,
  And sunk to their final resting-place.
Some have reached it in life's glad morn,
While the heart on Hope's waving wing was borne:
Escaped from the regions of care and sin,
They rest, ere the toils of their day begin.
Others have tasted of Pleasure's cup,
And have madly sought to quaff it up;
But the poison entered with stealthy creep,
And lulled to a long and fatal sleep.
Others have lived, and still lived on,
When hope and pleasure alike seemed gone;
Grief and anguish have torn the breast,
But all is over! and here they rest.
How hallowed a spot is the Christian's grave!
Nobly he stood in virtue brave,
Toiled and suffered, yet onward prest,—
Such as *his* be my long, last rest.

WRITTEN ON A MOTHER'S GRAVE.

PIRIT of my sainted mother !
   Haply now thy loved one near ;
To my heart thyself discover,
   Whisper there in accents dear.

Tell me I am not forsaken
   In this world of grief and pain ;
That thou still art near to bless me,
   Near to comfort and sustain.

Whilst upon the grave I 'm standing,
   Where thy sacred relics lie ;
Whilst upon the sod I 'm bending,
   Which conceals thee from my eye ;

Soft ! methinks I hear a whisper
   Breathing sweetly to my heart ;
Bidding me prepare to follow,
   And to meet thee where thou art.

Was it but a wild illusion
  Of the busy, restless brain ?
Dear deception ! sweet delusion !
  Still in memory's empire reign !

In my inmost soul abiding,
  Lead me through this wilderness
Till, the storms of life subsiding,
  I partake thy glorious bliss.

LINES WRITTEN IN SADNESS.

SO young, and yet so sad !
      Wherefore doth sorrow rest
      Within thy youthful breast ?
      Whilst all around is glad,
And nature in her loveliest robe is
      drest.

Nay ! weep not ! banish care !
Let nature's radiant smile
Lighten thine heart a while ;
This earth blooms bright and fair,
Then let its joy thy rising grief beguile.

Yet weep ! for this frail earth
Is fleeting as 'tis fair ;
Its loveliest things that are,—
Its hours of joy and mirth,
Its brightest hopes too soon yield to despair.

Is there no happier land—
Where sorrow hath no home,
Nor death nor blight may come,
To sweep with ruthless hand
Its brightest, fairest prospects, to the tomb ?

Beyond the flight of time
There is a brighter shore,
Where sorrow comes no more ;
A fadeless, happier clime ;
Where heavenly pleasures reign for evermore.

Then love not—prize not here,
What soon alas ! must die.
Earth's joys too quickly fly
To claim thy hope or fear :
Nothing below is worth a passing sigh.

THE QUEEN OF MAY.

THEY twined a wreath of roses,
    The freshest from the spray;
And bound them 'midst her clustering curls
    And crowned her Queen of May.
    The village maidens thronged around
With songs of artless glee,
And many a lovely form was found,
    But none so fair as she.

They have brought rich gems and radiant,
    To deck that polished brow,
And bound them 'midst those same bright curls
    Which droop in sadness now.
For Memory brings again the hour
    When her heart was light and gay,
And she pines for the well-known garden bower
    Where they crowned her Queen of May.

For the noble gallant at her side
    Hath won no willing hand;
And she hath but become his bride
    At her stern sire's command;

And her youth's bright dreams of happy hours
　　Have for ever flown away;
As transient though bright as the lovely flowers
　　That crowned her Queen of May.

They have bound a wreath of cypress
　　On that same snowy brow,
As it lies so cold and motionless,
　　For death hath triumphed now.
Her gentle spirit is at rest.
　　Is she not happier, say,
Than when earthly pleasure filled her breast,
　　As they crowned her Queen of May?

IN MEMORY OF A BELOVED CHILD.

TOO beautiful promise-bud! sweetly expand-
ing ;
Gladdening our hearts by thy freshness
and bloom ;
Ah! why so soon 'neath Life's piercing
blasts bending,
Why didst thou leave us, and sink to the tomb?

Was it that He who had bid thee to flourish
In earth's bleak garden-spot, saw that our love
Twined far too fondly round that which must perish,
And took the fair blossom to open above?

Yes! 'twas in love that thy charms first were granted,
Lighting our home with a beam from on high ;
And not less in love that those charms were transplanted
To bloom in the paradise-bowers of the sky.

Sweet tales of thy Saviour have often been told thee,
Thou hast learnt and delighted to warble His praise;
And now His loved arms shall for ever enfold thee,
And thy voice be attuned to the seraphim's lays.

And oh ! would one rebel-thought, rashly repining,
    Recall thee to earth from thy blissful abode ?
No ! no ! we will check them to trustful resigning,
    Nor question the infinite love of our God.

He lent thee, and decked thee with beauty and love,
    To show what fair beings surround Him on high ;
He recalled thee to draw our affections above,
    And centre our hopes with Himself in the sky.

DEATH'S VISITS.

DEATH entered a peaceful dwelling,
    Where a young and gentle pair
Were watching the bright outswelling,
    Of a blossom divinely fair;
Each day some new charm endeared
    The loved one to each fond heart,
Nor once had affection feared
    The stroke that should bid them part.
But a long, long night of sorrow,
    And the bright young form lies dead !
With streaming eyes, on the morrow
    They mourn life's hope-star fled.

Death passed to the halls resounding
    With voices of joy and mirth ;
And gay young hearts were bounding
    In the freshness and gladness of earth.
But hushed is the song that was lightest,—
    One dreadful, convulsive start—
The youngest—the fairest—the brightest—
    Hath felt the resistless dart.

A moment vainly contending,
    Friends strive 'gainst the weight of despair ;
Life's drama is suddenly ending,—
    The spirit is passing—ah ! where ?

Yet onward Death speeds unrelenting,
    And enters the busy scene,
Where, scheming, contriving, inventing,
    The man of the world is seen.
It hath touched him—the cherished treasures
    Fall from his nerveless sway ;
Friends—home—business—prospects—pleasures,
    Are rapidly passing away.
His accounts (save the dread one on high)
    Must be settled with feverish speed ;
Then closes for ever his eye,
    On his idol—the world—he is dead !

A holy and peaceful abode,
    Hallowed by praise and prayer,
Hath been rich in the blessing of God,
    But death hath a mission there.
The gifted,—the gentle,—the good,—
    Whose life was a ray of love,
A reflection of light on the road
    That leads to the mansions above.
High and noble had been her life's aim,
    And glorious was its decline ;
She passed, as in chariot of flame :
    Saviour ! grant such a death may be mine.

IN MEMORY OF A DEAR FRIEND.

AND is it so ? and art thou then departed,
        No more to dwell in this fair world below ?
    And was the tear that at our parting started
        But too prophetic of my future woe ?
    Fain would my heart, with fond affection
        beating,
    Hail thee with rapture at th' accustomed door ;
In vain had fancy pictured out that meeting :
    The place that knew thee once knows thee no more.
Oh ! say in what blest region doth thy spirit
    Calmly survey the scenes of former pain ?
What crown of glory dost thou now inherit ?
    And in what land of dazzling brightness reign ?
Ah ! little didst thou know the love I bore thee,
    The anguish that should fill my aching breast,
The tears that frail humanity shed o'er thee,
    Mourning thy entrance on eternal rest.
Cease, cease, fond heart ! thy sinful, vain repining ;
    And wish not *her* recall from yon bright shore :
A few short years, and, thy loved friend rejoining,
    O'er death triumphant we shall part no more.

A BIRTHDAY WISH.

BRIGHTLY the sunbeam chases the night,
Pouring rich treasures of beauty and light ;
Oh ! comes not a voice to thine heart from
 each ray,
 " Mayst thou have many happy returns of
  the day ?"

Sweet is the balmy breath of spring.
Rapturous the song of the bird on the wing ;
Seems not glad Nature around thee to say,
" Mayst thou have many happy returns of the day ?"

Hearts that love thee are breathing this morn,
Prayers on affection's wing upborne ;
To thy Father in heaven thy loved ones pray,
" Mayst thou have many happy returns of the day."

Sunshine must fade and the darkness come,
The beautiful spring yield to winter's gloom ;
But even when youth's fairy hopes decay,
" Mayst thou have many happy returns of the day."

May the love of thy Saviour with thee abide,
Be the word of thy Saviour thy counsel and guide ;
Thus walking in wisdom's pleasant way,
Thou shalt have many happy returns of the day.

There 's a land where purest pleasure reigns,
And praise resounds in celestial strains ;
Mayst thou, when thy heart and flesh decay,
There thank thy God for thy natal day.

TO THE NEW YEAR.

AIL! mysterious, viewless thing!
    With thy many-coloured wing;
    Come to bear us on our way;
    What thy solemn mission? —say!

One by one ye come and go,
Bearing us through joy and woe;
And whilst swiftly gliding by,
Leave your records in the sky.

New-born, untried year, I ask
What is *thine* allotted task?
Dost thou bring me hours of bliss?
Or the cup of wretchedness?

Will my path with love be crowned?
Tried and faithful friends surround?
Or, with torn and bleeding heart,
Must I from the loved ones part?

Shall I hear thy parting knell
As thou bid'st the earth farewell?
Or, art thou commissioned come
To consign me to the tomb?

Mortal! seek not thus to scan
Things revealèd not to man ;
Listen what thy Saviour taught—
" For the morrow take no thought."

Seek thou still to love thy God,
So shall all work for thy good ;
Ease or pain alike shall prove
Messengers of heavenly love.

Grief is joy, and smiles chase tears,
When His love the spirit cheers ;
Death is life.   The soul shall rise
Joyful to its native skies.

Hour by hour shall still unroll,
Slowly, my mysterious scroll ;
Fear not thou its lines to trace,
Fortified by sovereign grace.

Hide thee in thy Saviour's breast,
Only in His love seek rest ;
Thou shalt find me then to be
Fraught with happiness to thee.

THE SABBATH.

THROUGH the week the toiler, weary,
    Struggles on through griefs and fears.
With his prospects dark and dreary,
    For his eyes are dimmed with tears.
But a beam of heavenly glory,
    Dries the gushing tears away ;
Homeward, heavenward, rise his longings,
    On the blessed Sabbath-day.

'Midst the coming and the going
    Of the city's restless strife,
Scarce e'en breathing-time allowing,
    In the ceaseless whirl of life ;
What shall nerve the slave of business
    Still to plod his weary way ?
But the rest so calm and peaceful
    Of the blessed Sabbath-day.

Children, six sad days neglected,
    Roam through haunts of vice and sin ;
But the seventh, long expected,
    Dawns to call the wanderers in,—

THE SABBATH.

In, to mingle with the dear ones,
    Taught to love, and praise, and pray.
Oh, what charms to these young outcasts
    Hath the precious Sabbath-day !

By long contact with the cold world,
    Oh, how cold our hearts become !
Here we fold our wings, unheeding
    Of our everlasting Home.
But a fire burns in God's temple,—
    Cheered and quickened by its ray,
There we plume our wings for heaven
    On the hallowed Sabbath-day.

As—Creation's work completed,
    Fair, and bright, and pure it stood,
This sweet rest was first appointed
    By our wise and gracious God ;
So, when His six days of purpose
    Shall have slowly rolled away,
Then shall dawn the promised brightness
    Of an endless Sabbath-day.

ABSALOM.

ARK! the unusual sounds that greet the ear!
The trumpet's clangour and the din of war!
What mighty conflict 'pends, that thus the
    men
        Of Israel rise in arms, and take the field?
Have the proud Philistines again essayed
To dare the God of Jacob—to defy
The power of His anointed one, whose arm
Hath oft been strengthened for their overthrow?
Or hath the land of Syria poured her bands
To add the star of Jacob to the blaze
Of her proud coronet?   But stop! methinks
No alien I behold! and as they form
In battle's stern array, I mark a friend
Opposed to dearest friend!—Brother to brother!
Alas! what treacherous hand hath discord sown
T' embitter holy David's peaceful reign?
Who is yon leader of the rebel host,
Breathing defiance to his God and king?

Wonder of wonders!   Is it?   Can it be?
His Absalom? his own son Absalom?
The beautiful, enchanting Absalom?
The pride, the darling of his father's heart,
His best beloved—whom e'en in banishment
He yearned to see, and graciously restored
To favour—country—kindred—and to love?
Alas! 'tis he! rebellious Absalom!
But hark! he silence breaks, and gives command
Which flies throughout the host from man to man;
To all his captains thus the orders ran :—
Fear not! be valiant! for the day is ours!
Rewards shall crown the gallant and the brave!
Smite but the leader of yon little host,
Small, yet courageous, when engaged for *him*,
Their Prince; but when some fate-winged arrow
        strikes
And lays him low, they, like affrighted sheep,
Will scatter far and wide; and when the din
Of war hath passed away, will seek our sight,
And swear allegiance here.   'Twere pity that
So many of your brethren should be lost.
Smite only David!—let the rest escape.
He speaks.   And o'er his features, as he speaks,
(Those features once so beauteous; even now,
As there he sits on his well-mounted steed,
Who could conceive they hid such dire intent?)—
But o'er those features steals unearthly hate,
And on his brow defiance proudly sits,
Defiance hurled against his God—his king—
His father—and his country.   And his heart,

Inured to pride, and vice, and wickedness,
Recoils not at the foul and monstrous deed.
The heart turns sickening from the portrayed view
Of fallen man, and dread Satanic power.
But mark his aged sire ! oppressed with years,
And weight of griefs ; oppressed, yet not cast down,
For round him gather tried and faithful friends :
But not on these alone his trust is stayed.
His God is with him : and he stands secure
As in Jerusalem he was wont to stand.
He gives command.   And knowing well the day
Will turn for them, he orders them to spare
His erring son.   "Touch not the lad !" he cries,
And as the echo rings throughout the camp,
Again it swells, " Deal gently with my son."
But He whose high command is issued forth,
" Honour thy parents, that thy life be long,"
Had in His own Eternal Mind decreed
That erring Absalom's dark fate should teach
The awful truth to ages yet unborn,
That mighty though the prayers of godly sires
Or pleading mothers—yet e'en *they* shall fail
To screen the head of heaven-defying guilt.
Behold him, as he hangs on yonder tree !
Caught by his flowing locks so long his pride,
A spectacle for all.   'Twixt heaven and earth,
As though cast out, unfit alike for both.
Oh ! might we hope that in that brief reprieve
He sought and found forgiveness from his God
For his impiety.   But here the book
Of truth is silent, but this much reveals—

The sword of retributive justice fell
And pierced his heart, and he who madly sought
To wear a crown and build a lasting fame,
Fills a dishonoured grave, beneath a heap
Of monumental stones.

THE WIDOW'S LAMENT.

FAREWELL, beloved one! my heart's dearest
    treasure!
    Of all Heaven's gifts the most precious to
    me!
    Thine was affection and love beyond mea-
    sure,
How shall I tread earth's lone path without thee?

Oh! why doth memory, with too busy finger,
    Point to the visions that gild the bright past?
Why will my fond thoughts thus painfully linger
    On the blest moments too blissful to last?

Sleeping, I dream that thy voice of affection
    Chides the dark anguish corroding my breast;
Waking, I start to the sad recollection,
    In the dark grave thou hast found thy long rest.

I am alone in this cold world of sorrow,
    Wearily—hopelessly—life's path I tread;
Vainly would fond friends from earth's pleasures borrow
    Power to charm memories linked with the dead.

Nay ! not alone, mourner ; is it not written,
  " God to the widow a husband shall be ?"
Will He not bind up the heart He hath smitten ?
  Hath He not rich consolations for thee ?

Weep not the lost one—thou soon shalt regain him,
  Glorified, crowned with light, brighter than day ;
Wouldst thou again to this dark world enchain him,
  And prison his spirit in fetters of clay ?

Turn thy dimmed eye from the scene of earth's parting
  To the glad meeting that waits thee on high ;
Let the bright hope dry the tear that is starting :
  Thy loved one shall welcome thee home to the sky.

One is still with thee whose love is far stronger,
  And mightier His arm to protect and defend ;
Though shielded by earthly affection no longer,
  Thy Saviour remains—thy unchangeable Friend.

THE LAST OF THE FAMILY.

ESIDE a group of graves,
   In the village churchyard green;
In pensive sadness lingering there,
   A fair-haired boy was seen.

Not long had those graves been there,
   Scarce trodden the fresh-turned sod;
His parents had left him alone to the care
   Of kind friends and the orphan's God.

Unwonted bliss had shone
   On the home of his earliest days;
A halo of love round that household was thrown,
   And rare beauty adorned each face.

But a wail, long, loud, and deep,
   Startles the summer air;
The parents are gone to the grave to weep,
   For their youngest born lies there.

Her little pattering feet
　　Have ceased their merry dance ;
And her features smile in their rest as sweet
　　As if locked in blissful trance.

Scarce time had soothed the first
　　Wild throbbings of bitter woe,
When again a storm o'er the household burst,
　　And its earthly prop lay low.

A deeper, wilder groan
　　Was wrung from the mother's breast,
As the stay of her life—her cherished one—
　　Lay down in his wakeless rest.

The stroke too deeply fell
　　On the heart already riven ;
She bade her orphan boys farewell,
　　And passed away to heaven.

Again, with tearful eyes,
　　The mourners have sadly come,
The youngest and fairest of those bright boys
　　To lay in his little tomb.

And now the last stands there
　　Of that lovely family,
A boy of nine, with golden hair,
　　And earnest, thoughtful eye.

I clasped his little hand,
   And stroking his curling hair,
I spoke of the joys of that better land
   His dear ones were gone to share.

He showed me his father's grave,
   His mother's peaceful bed,
His brother's and sister's resting-place,
   And in cheerful accents said—

" Here lies my father dear,
   Here my mother by his side ;
And here they laid sweet Sarah Jane,
   And dear Tommy when he died.

" And here there yet is room,
   By my little brother's side,
To lay me too in a little grave,
   When I like them have died.

" Not long would I linger here,
   But hasten to those I love ;
Oh ! soon shall I meet them all again
   In our better home above."

Not long ! said the trusting child,
   And truly it was not long
Ere an added harp joined the angel choir.
   A glad spirit the blood-washed throng.

TO THE SEA-GULLS.

BIRDS of the tireless wing,
   Fearlessly traversing
     Over the deep;
   Your pathway wild and bright,
   Feel ye not strange delight
As on your pinions light
   Onward ye sweep?

Dauntless and free ye roam
Over the billowy foam
   Of the green sea.
Happy your trackless reign,
Far spread your wide domain
From the abodes of man,
   Boundless and free.

Birds of the waving wing!
Who guides your wandering
   O'er the vast flood?

He who from heaven's far height
Marketh the sparrow's flight
Hath even you in sight,
    Nature's great God.

Free on your tireless wing
As the imagining
    Of some wild dream ;
Riding the waves in mirth,
Beings not chained to earth,
Of a far nobler birth,
    Sea-birds ye seem.

So would my spirit soar,
Chained down to earth no more,
    Happier to dwell ;
Like you would I arise,
Soar to my native skies,
Bid these fleet vanities
    One long farewell.

"THE HOARY HEAD IS A CROWN OF GLORY."

ANY sing in joyful measures
  Of youth, bright youth ;
Of its transports and its pleasures,
  Of its love and its truth.
But is there not rich blessing
Crowns life's last stage—
The honour of possessing
  A good old age ?

Oh ! I love the crown entwining
  The old man's brow ;
Those silvery locks are shining
  With rich glory now :
They tell of many a combat
  In life's pilgrimage ;
All honour to the victor
  Crowned with bright old age !

From the turmoil and the worry
  Of life's long day,
From its bustle and its hurry
  He turns now away.
And holier contemplations
  His rapt soul engage,
And heavenly aspirations
  Cheer calm old age.

And children round him listen
  With fixed, anxious look,
As he readeth many a lesson
  From memory's full book.
Oh, precious, as he turneth
  Over page by page,
Is the lore that childhood learneth
  From wise old age.

And his spirit strength will gather
  From the years long gone,
As he thinketh of the Father
  Who hath still led him on.
For he knoweth that the promises
  To bless him still engage,
And he witnesseth God's faithfulness
  The same to hoary age.

Now his outward sense is failing,
  And his eyes grow dim ;

But to inward ear is swelling
  The seraphs' holy hymn.
And angels ope the portal,—
  From life's last stage
He wakes to youth immortal
  From blest old age.

ON SEEING THE CORPSE OF A SISTER.

FAREWELL, beloved one! 'tis hard to sur-
render
 One faithful friend when this world yields
  so few ;
 Thine was affection so pure and so tender,
  Gentle, unwavering, constant, and true.

Yet I will dwell not in sinful repining
 On my great loss—'tis thine infinite gain ;
Yonder thy glorified spirit is shining,
 Meet with thy blessed Redeemer to reign.

Faith lends its aid, and earth's shadows dispelling,
 Points my lone heart to a mansion of rest,
Where in the sunshine of love thou art dwelling,
 Safe with thy Jesus, and lodged in His breast.

Long years of sorrow may now lie before me,
 And thy voice no longer my troubles allay ;
But no ! my sweet sister ! I will not deplore thee :
 Thy God shall be mine, and thy Saviour my stay.

TO MY FATHER.

WELCOME, thy natal day!
 Father! our fond hearts say ;
  May it be blest !
 Still, as they go and come,
 Marking thy pathway home,
May they bring visions
 Of heavenly rest !

Long have thy footsteps trod
Over life's changing road,
 God for thy guide ;
Still may His love attend,
Still may His power defend,
Still to thy journey's end
 In Him confide.

Ere called to thy reward,
Mayst thou long years be spared,
 Is our heart's prayer ;
And when, as one by one
We lay life's burden down,
Round yonder dazzling throne
 We 'll meet thee there.

TO THE SAME.

GAIN, O long-forgotten Muse, thy sacred
influence bring,
Attune my heart to minstrelsy, and strike
each trembling string.
First, let a burst of praise arise, which God
shall deign to hear,
Whose love hath spared my honoured sire through yet
another year.
Still, O Thou All-indulgent Power! in rich abundance
shed
Blessings divine from hour to hour upon his honoured
head.
And, father dear! as once again fond Memory takes
her stand,
And, gazing o'er the busy past, waves her enchanted
wand;
And whilst obedient to her call the thronging visions
rise,
In panoramic vividness, before thy streaming eyes,
Visions of youth, with all its joys, and cares of riper
years;

Faces now changed by time or death, clouds, sunshine,
    hopes, and fears :
Oh ! whilst reviewing thus the past, dost thou not ever
    find
True to His Word thy Covenant God, the faithful, good,
    and kind !
And whilst the past so loudly calls for gratitude and
    praise,
Will He not guide thy feeble steps through life's re-
    maining days !
Lean in thy weakness on His strength, cast on Him all
    thy care,
Thy pardoning, loving, gracious God, will all thy bur-
    dens bear.
So guided by His providence, supported by His grace,
He who *hath* kept thee still shall keep, till thou behold
    His face.
May we, the children of thy prayers, the children of thy
    love,
Rejoin thee in yon blest abode, our better home above !

VOICE OF THE NEW YEAR.

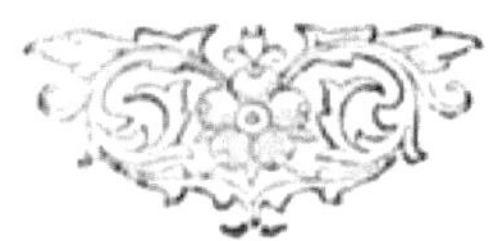ORTAL! my moments are quickly fleeting;
   They come—they are gone for ever,
The heart where life's pulses are warmest
     beating
   Soonest from life may sever.
I come, with seasons of Gospel-grace,
   By sovereign love bestowed,
With whispers of peace to a guilty race;
Then hasten the offered boon to embrace,
   And live this year for thy God.

LINES SUGGESTED BY THE LAKE SCENERY OF WINDERMERE.

AND can it be that this sin-tainted earth
     Can boast of scenes of grandeur such as
        this,
     Scenes that to holiest, purest thoughts give
        birth,
  Where the heart revels in a wondrous bliss?
Hath not the curse yet touched this favoured spot?
And have I found a place where its dread influence
    reacheth not?

Long pent-up feelings rush in whelming tide
    Over my spirit with resistless power;
Visions of youth to-day with me abide—
    Wafting my thoughts to happier days of yore;
And once again renew, as when a child,
My communings with Nature's voices, deep, and grand,
    and wild.

Read we not here, as in an open book,
    The teachings of Jehovah's love and power?

'Twas from His hand their form these mountains took,
   And the same hand bestows the verdant dower
Of loveliness upon these sleeping vales.
His power sustains the universe ! His goodness never
     fails !

How oft hath contemplation dipt her pen
   In inspiration drawn from this sweet place!
And wondrous thoughts, and burning words, have then
   Left on the page their never-dying trace.
Thoughts that have lodged in many a wayward breast,
Winning it back to paths of peace, and purity, and rest.

And here shall many a gifted one again
   Drink at this fount of beauty ; till each sense,
Entranced in visions passing mortal ken,
   Is borne away from earth's enchantments hence,
To give us glimpses of yon world of light,
Where one eternal summer reigns—one Sabbath pure
     and bright.

TO HEALTH.

TELL me where thou dwellest,
    Choicest boon of earth,
Lightener of our sorrow,
    Heightener of our mirth.

Laughing in the bright beam
    Of the joy-lit eye,
Touching into beauty
    Cheeks of roseate dye.

Filling life with transport ;
    Tuning earth to song ;
Scattering hope's bright blossoms
    Darkest paths among.

Tell me where thou dwellest,
    There too would I dwell,
Or on mountain's wild top,
    Or in shady dell.

Mortal ! wouldst thou woo me ?
  Come in early morn ;
Drink the balmy perfume
  On soft breezes borne.

Talk with waking nature,
  As she springs to light,
Clad in radiant beauty,
  From the lap of night.

Chase me o'er the hill-top,
  Where the wild winds play ;
Seek me by the streamlet,
  Glittering on its way.

Leave the chains of fashion,
  Leave the giddy throng ;
Spend not night's sweet rest-hours
  Crowded halls among.

Seek not costly dainties,
  Let thy wants be few ;
Follow Wisdom's teachings,
  Holy, pure, and true.

Leave the sparkling wine-cup,
  Ruddy though it gleams ;
Drink the Heaven-sent nectar
  Of the crystal streams.

Seek, and thou shalt find me,
  Smiling health shall come,
Showering priceless blessings
  On thy heart and home.

THE WINDS.

INDS! gentle summer winds! sportive and
     free,
Rippling the streamlet and stirring the tree;
Scattering the fragrance of blossom and
     flower—
Filling with perfume the sweet shady bower,
Fanning the cheek in the hot sultry air,
Winds! summer winds! how delightful ye are!

Winds! autumn winds! how ye fitfully moan!
Wakening strange memories of dreams that are flown;
Wantonly scattering the leaves far and wide,
That ye lately caressed in their bright summer pride.
Oh! as things beautiful die all around,
Wild winds of autumn, how mournful ye sound!

Winds! tempest winds! in wrath shaking your chain!
Flinging destruction and death in your train!
Grasping the oak that for ages has grown,
And with force irresistible whirling it down.
Making the stoutest heart quail 'neath your power,—
Fierce tempest winds! how terrific your roar!

Winds! angry winds! that in passionate sweep
Stir up the ocean, and lash up the deep!
Tossing the bark on the foam-crested wave—
Dashing her down to a dark, unknown grave!
Oh! as we breathe for the seaman a prayer,
Winds, in your wild gusts, how dirge-like ye are!

INTEMPERANCE—A VISION.

RAPPED up in vision, strange sights I
    saw,
Filling my soul with a whelming awe :
A hideous monster trod the ground,
Each step flung ruin and death around,
Blighting the fairest flowers of earth,——
Crushing Hope's buds at their happy birth,
Quenching the love-lights of heart and home,--
Sweeping the slain to the dark, deep tomb.

I saw in my vision a happy hearth ;
One of the holiest spots of earth.
Father and mother and children fair,
Dwelt, oh, how sweetly and peacefully there !
But the monster came with unpitying eye,
And blotted the sun from their household sky :
He breathed on the sire with his pestilent breath,
And existence henceforth was a living death.
Dead to the wife of his heart he became—
Dead to his children in all but name.

Those lately clasped in his fond embrace
Now fled in affright from his sin-stamped face.
The household idols, one by one,
Years' hoarded treasures, were widely strewn.
The home he had reared in his youth's bright
     hour
Lay blighted and cursed by the demon's power.
And happiness, comfort, and plenty fled,
And reason, and honour, and love seemed dead.
Till his murderous arm the death-stroke dealt
On the suffering wife at his feet who knelt ;
And the wail of despair rang a wild death-knell,
As a sable pall o'er the picture fell.

My vision changed, and, young and fair,
A bridal party were standing there ;
A maiden adorned with winning grace,
And the love-smile lighting her blushing face,
With downcast eye and trembling voice,
Gave heart and hand to the youth of her choice,
And their mutual vows of changeless love
Were registered there and recorded above.
From the sacred shrine in joy and pride
He led to his home his lovely bride,
And that sweet word "home," to his ear became
A hallowed and talismanic name,
Nerving his arm and inspiring his heart
In life's great drama to act his part.
Long months of unclouded happiness
Mellowed their love and increased their bliss,
And a darling babe to their arms was given,

Bright as the cherubs that people heaven.
And so great was their joy in that proud, glad
  hour,
That it seemed as if nought but death had power
To scatter their dream of happiness,
Or dash from their lips the cup of bliss.
But the deadly foe came even there,
And cast his spell o'er that mother fair.
Oh! direful spell! not the desert blast—
The dread simoom, as it sweepeth past,
Could ruin work more foul and fell
Than was wrought in that home by that cursed
  spell!
It swept the dignity from her face—
It withered each charm and it banished each
  grace,
It dashed the purity from her brow,
And the brand of guilt it weareth now.
Forgotten was all that had formed a part
Of each thought and each throb of her love-tuned
  heart;
Forgotten the sacred duties of wife,
Forgotten the babe she had loved as her life;
Forgotten the pride of an honoured name,
Forgotten all! all! but sin and shame!
Too heavy the grief and too cruel the dart
For the tender, woe-stricken husband's heart.
The life-cord snapped, and the silent tomb
Gave him his last remaining home.
God shield the babe! in its helplessness left,
By the demon of parents and home bereft.

Again a change o'er my vision past,
There was laughter and song and a merry feast.
A lovely boy, and the only son—
The darling—the cherished—the precious one—
The joy of his mother—his father's pride,
Was there ; and they welcomed his natal tide.
Passing from childhood into youth,
His lips spoke love and his eyes beamed truth.
Heir to a rich ancestral dower,
But heir to the mind's far nobler store.
His fair bright boyhood full promise gave
Of the man—frank, noble, generous, brave.
But the fiend was there in secret guise,
And gazed on his victim with serpent eyes ;
And the gaze with fascinating art
Hath charmed the young, unsuspecting heart.
And the coils round the beautiful boy are thrown
That shall drag him to hopeless ruin down.
In the sparkling red of the tempting glass
There lurketh a deadly power, alas !
Which shall quench the last sparks of earthly hope
In the stealthy and deadly poison cup.
Years sped from the night of that festive joy,
But where is that lovely and blooming boy ?
Gone are the friends of his early youth !—
Gone the bright beamings of love and truth !—
Gone are the guides of his happier years,
His parents are gone from a world of cares.
Gone the ancestral proud domains—
Darkness and desolation reigns
Where the rays of love and the beams of mirth

Had illumined the fairest spot of earth.
Where is he? ask the besotted throng
That startle night with the reveller's song!
Their degrading haunts he long hath known,
But, alas! he is farther, and deeper gone!
Where is he? ask the few who watch
The last faint sigh of the dying to catch,
But start as a strength-restoring hour
Revives the disease of maddening power,
And groans and shrieks shake with dire alarm
The hearts and the hands that would shield him from
    harm,
Till a mightier hand stops the labouring breath
And the lips are sealed by the touch of death.
And the monster, unsatisfied, turns away
To seek, and ensnare, and devour other prey.

I saw in my vision till earth was red
With the life-blood the foul destroyer shed;
And I heard in my vision deep groans that rose,
Like expiring nature's wild death throes;
Scarcely a home but *his* wand had touched—
Scarcely a hope but *his* hand had crushed;
Rich, poor, wise, ignorant, old and young,
Were slain in one undistinguished throng,
And cast in a dark dishonoured grave—
And I cried aloud for some hand to save.
And I saw, with wonder-stricken eyes,
A noble, majestic figure rise!
Awaked by the groans of deep despair
That wildly filled the resounding air.

With lion heart, and unconquered might,
BRITANNIA rose to assert her right.
She saw the foe that ravaged her land,
And grasped her sceptre with firmer hand.
And the pure, clear light of her flashing eye
Darted like sunbeam from summer sky.
And the awe-struck thousands crowded round,
As she stood with beauty and glory crowned.
With upraised arm and resistless stroke
The spell and the power of the tyrant she broke ;
And the shouts of the thousands rent the skies
As the monster fell, no more to rise.
And the spreading joy made my glad heart dance
Till its throbbings dispelled my blissful trance.

But alas ! not in vision, but truth, I found
The spoils of Intemperance spread around.
The ruined home and the blighted name—
The shattered peace and the blasted fame ;—
But amidst the dark and deepening gloom,
A ray of hope to my heart has come.
That my vision, with true prophetic eye,
Looks to the time approaching nigh,
When Justice and Liberty, hand-in-hand,
Shall work the deliverance of our land ;
And the God-own'd Temperance cause assert
Its reign in each home and its power in each heart.

DIALOGUE.

A MOUNTAIN AND A MOLEHILL.

ANN.—Good morning, Janet! have you heard
    the strange news?
If not, to believe it I fear you'll refuse,
Squire Simms's large meadow has seen a
    strange sight,
A mountain has risen up during the night.

Janet.—A mountain has risen, you say?

Ann.—Yes! just so,
Such wonderful things have happened, you know,
Ellen Jones has assured me that such was the case.

Janet.—Well! if so, I will hasten at once to the place.

Ann.—Yes, do; you will find it, no doubt, as I say.
I can't go just now, so will wish you "Good-day."

Janet.—Well, Ellen! what wonders are these you
    have seen?

Ellen.—Oh! the hill that has risen at Oak Farm,
    you mean?

Janet.—Not a hill, but a mountain's the tale that I
    heard,
Which Ann Ellis declared came from you word for word.

Ellen.—I never named mountain, she very well knows,
She would add a bit to it herself, I suppose.
I've not been myself yet to see it, but still
I have heard on good grounds 'twas a very large hill.
Betsy Mason met crowds of folks running to see;
I wonder indeed what the cause on 't can be!

Janet.—Well, I think, as I 'm more than a mile on
    my track,
I'll go forward and see it before I go back;
Whether mountain or hill it will much surprise me,
Such a wonderful sight in our country to see.

Janet.—Well, Betsy, and have you returned from Oak
    Farm?
I hope the strange earthquake has done no great harm.
Pray what size is the hill? I've been straining my eyes,
But can see nothing of it. How high does it rise?

Betsy.—An earthquake? A hill? Pray what do you
    mean?
I assure you nor earthquake nor hill *I* have seen.

Janet.—Ellen Jones said——

Betsy.—Oh! now I begin to perceive,
How foolish you must be *her* tale to believe.
I merely just said that I met on my way
Mary Parker, who told me she heard yesterday
That a cartload of earth was thrown up in a night
In Squire Simms's large field.   'Twas a curious sight;
I did think of just going as far to inquire,
But with stopping to tell folks, I've let out my fire;
And our John will be back from his work very soon,
For the time's swiftly passing, and soon 'twill be noon.
But perhaps if you're taking the trouble to learn,
You'll call and enlighten me as you return.

Janet.—Well! here I have come four or five miles
        to-day,
On a most foolish errand I'm sorry to say.
A mountain reduced to a very large hill—
Then the hill to no more than a waggon would fill!
I declare I don't think it at all worth my while
To go any farther, though 'tis but a mile.
And yet for *a cartload of earth* to appear,
Is strange, if 'tis true, so now I *am* here,
I'll e'en see the end on 't, so wish you " Good-day,"
Very likely I shan't be returning this way.
And now here I am—but wherever I turn
Nor mountain, nor hillock, my eye can discern.
How vexing to think what a fool I must be,
When, in place of a mountain, there's nothing to see

But Will Sharlock, the ploughman.   He 's coming this
    way,
I 'll tell him, and see what the old man will say.
Oh, William, has any strange sight here been seen ?

William.—No, nought as I know on.   But wot don
    yo mean ?

Janet.—Why, I heard that a mountain rose here in
    a night,
And I 've travelled near six miles to see the strange
    sight,
But various stories I 've heard with surprise—
The mountain reduced to a large hill in size,
Then the hill to a cartload of earth ; but I fear
'Tis a hoax, for there 's nothing to see now I 'm here.

William.—Yi, there 's summat to see ; just step this
    way, Miss ;
Here 's a hill for yo ; did you e'er see aught like this?

Janet.—A hill ?   Yes, a molehill.   I 've seen those
    before.

William.—Well, that 's yer great mountain—ye 'll see
    nothing more.
Aw con tell in a minnit how th' tale 's getten out.
Aw seed Parker's little lass playing about,
An aw towd her aw 'd show her a wonderful seet,
A heap o' fresh earth wot had risen in th' neet.

So hoo run to her mother, un th' tale ut hoo towd,
Loike a snowbo geet bigger, as farther it rolled ;
Un neaw, if yo'n listen wot aw 've geet to say
Aw 'll engage yer walk shannot be quite thrown away.
As long as yo live ne'er believe idle chat—
" He says," and " Hoo towd me," an rubbish like that.
A tale set a-goin is just loike a stone
Thrown into a pond, and we see, one by one,
The circles geet bigger and bigger all round,
Till at last they reach out to the sides of the pond.
Whatever you say, let strict truth rule your tongue
And keep close to plain sense, an' yo 'll not go far wrong.

LINES ON THE LOSS OF THE BRIG *FAVOURITE* OFF BLACKPOOL.

 OT *one* to tell the tale of that dread night?
    Alas! not one? Couldst thou, O greedy
        sea!
    Engulf them thus, with land and friends
        in sight,
To enhance death's wild and bitter agony?
Whilst yearning crowds in terror throng the beach,
To see them perish—just beyond their reach!

How gaily sped the bark from Afric's shore,
    Laden with costly wares;—but costlier far
The precious living freight that vessel bore,
    The noble heart of each brave fearless tar;
Proudly she ploughed her way across the wave,
And rode the billows, soon to be her grave.

Past were the perils of the shoreless deep;
    Rejoicingly they near the land once more;

But the death angel's wing broods dark and deep.
  What means that shock ?   Alas ! all, all is o'er !
All but the orphans' cries and widows' groans—
God of the friendless, bless the stricken ones !

ADIEU.

DIEU! How mournful the sound! How
tenderly melancholy the reflections it awak-
ens! What breast unseared by crime and
guilt but feels a lively chord vibrate as the
touching accents fall upon the ear, which
probably have often been re-echoed from the depths
of an affectionate and sorrowful heart? They bring
back to one, perchance, the image of a friend whose
counsel and whose company was once precious, con-
soling, and elevating; but who, amidst the changing
scenes of life's pilgrimage, has been removed—perhaps
by distance, perhaps by death—from our sight and
hearing. Oh, those last parting moments! Those
hearts almost too full for utterance! How vividly memory paints again the scene! How cherished—how
hallowed the word in which the feelings of the bosom at
length found vent—the scarcely audible, yet fervently
breathed "Adieu!" Perchance to another it brings
again the last moments of a departing parent. His
children gather around his bed, mournfully gazing on
those features which have so often beamed on them with

looks of unutterable tenderness, but upon which now
the cold damps of death are set.   For the last time they
have heard that voice of trusting supplication, invoking
that gracious Providence, which hath been his support
through life, to take his loved ones, soon to be father-
less, into its special protection.   The last parental blessing has been given ; and now, as he feels the awful crisis
approaching, he summons up his remaining strength to
pronounce the solemn " Adieu !"   Oh, with what bursting tears, or with what heartrending, silent grief, are
the last accents heard to fall from those honoured lips !
And how, even at the lapse of many years, will the
wound again open and the heart bleed afresh at the
sound of the word " Adieu !"

Or perhaps a beloved child has shared for many years
the sacred, fostering influences of a happy home ; but
the parting hour has arrived.   The links that time had
so firmly welded, with ruthless hand he now tears
asunder : and the hour approaches that separates the
nearest and tenderest ties.   The youth leaves the home
of his childhood—the spot around which centre his
holiest and purest thoughts—the scene of his first and
sweetest earthly enjoyments, to enter on a new and untried world.   Hope, with her fairy wand, conjures up
visions of splendour to gild the future ; and perchance
he dreams that happiness awaits him, even greater than
that he leaves.   He understands not the mournful expression of his father's countenance, as he gives him his
counsel and blessing ; nor the tears that choke a fond
mother's utterance as the word " Adieu !" trembles on
her lip.   But after long years, should he be spared, will

that parting scene recur to his mind. Fortune may have smiled on him; but less bright will her smiles appear than those he met in childhood. The laurel of fame may deck his brow, and virtue herself crown that brow with purity and lustre; yet still the " Adieu!" which he bade to home will sound to his heart, as memory whispers it, as the knell of his sweetest hopes and most unmixed joys.

How varied the emotions! How multitudinous the scenes which this brief word serves to awaken! And how the heart turns from the contemplation of the separations and bereavements of earth to that bright land where its sound shall never more be heard—where friendships shall never be dissolved—where death shall never enter—and where partings and tears are unknown!

GOOD-BYE.

HOSE lips have not breathed the familiar old
    word,
  Often carelessly uttered and carelessly heard ?
  What various scenes to these accents give
    birth !
'Midst sadness and sorrow—'midst laughter and mirth,
With the light buoyant tone, or the heart-wringing sigh,
We have spoken or wept out the old word "Good-bye."

There are times when the heart is too heavy to speak,
When the eloquent flush mantles high on the cheek.
In one moment seem pent up the feelings of years,
And no vent can be found save the language of tears ;
Unbidden they rush to the tale-telling eye,
And choke the fond voice that would whisper "Good-
    bye."

When the outward-bound vessel is leaving the shore,
And fond hearts are severing that *may* meet no more,
And the eye of affection is straining to trace

For the last time the features of each beloved face—
Between them must soon the dark ocean wave lie ;
Oh ! the heart-breaking anguish of that last "Good-
    bye."

And though miles and not seas our lot may divide
From fond loving hearts, long trusted and tried ;
Yet the gladness of meeting is checked by the pain
Of the thought that before we may greet them again,
Long months or long years may roll wearily by—
Oh ! how mournfully sad is the lingering "Good-bye."

Yet, though here oft divided from those that we love,
A blissful re-union awaits us above ;
There kindred souls dwell in unsullied delight,
And in love's happy circle for ever unite.
In our beautiful home that awaits us on high,
No partings shall wring the reluctant " Good-bye."

SUNSHINE.

SUNSHINE on the mountain,
    And the merry dancing rill,
Bursting its ice-locked fountain,
    Leaps sparkling down the hill;
And a thousand diamond flashes
  Reflect the welcome ray,
As the streamlet onward dashes
  On its fertilising way.

Sunshine in the dale,
  And the re-awakening flowers
Bespread the grassy vale
  And bedeck the rosy bowers ;
And a thousand warbling voices
  Their happy welcome sing,
And glad Nature now rejoices
  In the smile of new-born spring.

Sunshine round the hearth,
  Where the tender love-light beams,
And affection gushes forth,
  Like unfettered mountain streams ;

And the cold world's icy crust
  Thaws 'neath the genial ray,
And chill harshness and distrust
  Melt like winter snows away.

Sunshine in the heart,
  Shrouded long in sorrow's night ;
For Hope's golden flashes dart
  A soul-reviving light :
And sweet sympathetic words,
  And love's resistless power,
Touch the bosom's hidden chords,
  Wakening melody once more.

Oh ! the past hath had its gloom,
  For the heart as for the eye ;
But we hail the time of bloom,
  And the sunshine from on high.
And though like a pleasing story
  These summer days depart,
Be ours a fadeless glory—
  The sunshine of the heart.

A SAD SIGHT.

ROSTRATE on the cold ground he lay,
   A piteous sight to see ;
His cheek was furrowed, his hair was grey,
   A worn old man was he.

Alone he lay on the frozen ground,
   His hat had rolled from his brow,
And soon might those silvery locks be bound
   With a wreath of whiter snow.

What cruel hand hath dealt the blow,
   And left him there to die ?
Or what fell stroke hath laid him low,
   When no helping hand was nigh ?

Alas ! the foe that hath wrought him woe
   In his bosom hath been nursed ;
He hath madly quaffed the poison cup,
   Which hath done the deed accursed.

'Tis sad to see the young succumb
  To the power of the hideous foe ;
But the worn old man on the brink of the tomb,
  Is a sadder sight, I trow.

For the wisdom years should have treasured up,
  To gild life's sunset hour,
Hath been quenched in the dread Circean cup
  Of fatal, deadly power.

And the laurels that crown the silvery head
  Are trampled 'neath withering scorn ;
Wearily—vainly—his life hath sped—
  He hath only gathered the thorn.

What fathomless tale of dark, deep woe,
  Lies hid in that man's career !
How hearts that love him have bled ere now
  For him who lies weltering there.

God of the noble Temperance band,
  All other hopes seem fled ;
On the poor drunkard lay Thine hand,
  And raise as from the dead.

A HOLIDAY SONG.

WAY ! away ! 'tis a glad, free day,
  And a thousand hearts beat light and gay :
  And old Care throws his burden off for
    a while,
  And his wrinkles yield to the beaming smile.

Away ! away ! for the earth is gay,
And puts on her holiday dress to-day ;
And sylvan solitudes start at the sound
Of the joyous throngs that invade the ground.

Away ! away ! from the dusty street,
To where mossy carpets await the feet ;
Away ! from the whirl of the busy mill,
To the peaceful murmurs of brook and rill.

Away ! from the din of the crowded mart,
To where heaven-sent whispers may teach the heart :
To read in the glory and beauty of earth,
His wisdom and goodness who gave them birth.

Away ! and roam o'er the green hill-side,
By the inland stream, or the flowing tide ;—
Health, beauty, and gladness await ye to-day—
Then join in the jubilant holiday.

TO JOHNNY, ON WEARING HIS FIRST SUIT.

YOUNG voyager! thus early cast
   On life's tempestuous, stormy sea;
Leaving behind in eager haste
   The badge of infancy.

No monarch in his robes of state
   Feels greater pride than swells thy breast,
In tiny man's attire complete
   Thus to be dressed.

How little know'st thou, daring one,
   The dangers that before thee lie;
What veils of darkness may be thrown
   Across thy sky.

Oh, could we read the burning thought
   That kindles in thine earnest eye—
What visions with the future fraught
   Before thee lie!

How wide expands thy little heart,
  Reaching beyond its present span !
On life's great stage to act *thy* part,
    And be a man.

Go, then, and gird thine armour on,
  Fear not to trust the billows dark :
In fiercest storms there still is One
    Can guide thy bark.

Oh, mayst thou early learn His fear !
  Oh, mayst thou early feel His love !
Live 'neath His smile and blessing here,
    Then find thy home above !

THE GATE OF HEAVEN.

I T was a lovely Sabbath afternoon,
    That found me by a couch, whereon there
        lay
    One passing gently—peacefully away,
    Away from earth's dark mists to heaven's un-
        clouded noon.

A noble brow was hers, whereon sat throned
    A dignity that spoke a nobler mind,
    Cultured, and intellectual, and refined;
A heart which virtue ruled, and love had sweetly
        toned.

A group were gathered in that peaceful room,
    Where it had almost seemed a sin to weep;
    So calm she looked, as if on point to sleep:
But ah! a long, long sleep in the cold silent tomb.

And one stood there, who, with a father's pride,
    Had watched each opening charm bloom and ex-
        pand,

Now to be nipped by death's relentless hand :
The grief which wrung his heart he strove in vain to
    hide.

As if the sound had kindled up anew
    The lamp of life, and broken the sweet trance
    That rapt her spirit, as her heavenward glance
Seemed fixed on wondrous things, hidden from mortal
    view.

She turned on him her tender, loving eyes,
    Lit with celestial radiance from above,
    And sought with words of holy faith and love
To dry his gushing tears, and still the bursting sighs.

" Cease, my fond father, causelessly to mourn
    That my life's race so quickly hath been run,
    And I so early hear the glad ' Well done '—
Thou soon shalt come to me, though I may not return.

" A brighter lot than thou, with all thy care,
    Couldst e'er have woven for me, now is mine :
    Rejoicingly earth's pleasures I resign,
Angels are beckoning—and I haste their bliss to share.

" Kind hast thou been, my father, ever kind,
    My love grows stronger as life's moments wane ;
    And now the only thought that gives me pain
Is thus to leave thee sad and sorrowing here behind.

" Think, O my father, think and weep no more,
How great the honour that to thee is given ;
Thy sainted children waiting thee in heaven—
Waiting to greet thee home to yon immortal shore.

" And couldst thou—wouldst thou keep me suffering
here ?
Now, while bright visions of unspoken things,
And lovely seraphs with their shining wings,
Woo my glad spirit hence to an immortal sphere ? "

The father's burst of anguish deep and wild
Was checked.   Triumphant faith his bosom fired :
His tears were dried ; his heart with praise inspired ;
He blessed the Hand that gave and took his darling
child.

TO MY HUSBAND, ON HIS BIRTHDAY.

VER coming, ever going,
   So life's changing years roll on,
Like the wild wave's ceaseless flowing,
   Coming—going—one by one.

Many thus have left their traces
   Deeply graven on thine heart ;
Ever-varying scenes and faces
   Up to memory's vision start.

And another lies before thee
   As a sealed and solemn book ;
And its destinies hang o'er thee ;—
   Who into its depths may look ?

Wisely hid from our beholding
   Lies its dark and mystic scroll ;
Hour by hour its page unfolding
   Shall each changing scene unroll.

But affection breathes a prayer, love,
　　That, of all past years the best,
Untold blessings it may bear, love,
　　Daily—hourly—to thy breast.

Cheered by hope, and soothed by peace, love,
　　Mayst thou fearless tread life's road ;
Find thy rest when life shall cease, love,
　　In the palace of thy God.

ON RECEIVING MY BROTHER'S CARTE DE VISITE.

ARVELLOUS power, and wondrous art,
Thus to give to the eye and the heart
The life-like image and faithful trace
Of the long-lost form and the long-loved face.

Though years of change and untiring time,
And the ocean wave and the far-off clime,
Have hidden thee from me as once thou wert,
Yet here I behold thee as now thou art.

Time, my brother, hath touched thy brow,
And an anxious look it weareth now ;
He hath shaken his wing o'er thy glossy hair,
And silvery glory is gathering there.

And many a dream of thy youth is fled,
And many a cherished hope is dead ;
And many a friend of the distant yore
Thou shalt see and greet on earth no more.

K

But cheer, my brother ; with trust in Heaven,
Grasp the bright hopes to thee yet given :—
Though not so dazzling, yet far more true,
Than the pictures imagination drew.

Rest on thy God thy troubled soul :
Yield to thy Saviour's sweet control :
Seek but His will—His glory—His grace—
Trust where blind Nature fails to trace.

Lean not to earth—'tis a broken reed !
Labour in faith—God give thee speed !
Be Jesus thy constant, present Friend.
All shall be well in the glorious end.

THE VOYAGE OF LIFE.

SAILING on—ever on—
    Down the stream of time :
Lulled to rest, on its breast,
    By a ceaseless chime.—
Hours departing, fresh ones starting
In their course sublime.

Sailing on—ever on—
    See the new-launched bark !
Gentle wave, lightly lave
    That frail little ark ;
Quench not quite Life's faint light,
    Spare the tiny spark !

Sailing on—ever on—
    Through Youth's happy dream ;
Banks of bowers, trees and flowers,
    Deck the fairy scene.
Oh, how bright ! oh, how light !
    Do the winged hours seem,

Sailing on—ever on—
  Many a changing year
Leaves its trace on the face—
  Furrowed o'er with care.
Bright hopes flown.—Still sail on,
  No abiding here.

Sailing on—ever on—
  Through the snows of age ;
Silvery hair, blanched with care,
  And the wild storm's rage.
Still sail on— swiftly on
  Yet another stage.

Sailing on—ever on—
  Where ? oh, where is He !
Ends Life's dream—ends Time's stream
  In a boundless sea.
Ask no more ! none may explore
  Dread Eternity.

ANNIE.

A SIMPLE LIFE SKETCH.

'TWAS the early time of autumn, ere the russet
    tinged the leaves,
    Ere the yellow, ripening harvest was ga-
    thered into sheaves,
    'Twas the lovely sunset hour, when a mel-
    low radiance streams,
Decking earth with witching loveliness, such as decks
    childhood's dreams.
A fair and gentle maiden sat pensive and alone,
Wrapt in melancholy musings on the bliss too sadly
    flown ;
For the budding spring had brought her hope's bright
    blossoms fresh and gay,
But the early autumn taught her how things lovely
    pass away.
She had heard the first glad breathings of love's im-
    passioned sigh,
She had read affection beaming from another's earnest
    eye ;

He was all her fancy pictured—she was all he sought
    to gain,
And their hearts seemed bound together, as with
    adamantine chain.
Lovely in mind and person was Annie Campbell fair,
Gentle in tone and manner, with a brow of earnest care;
For a soul-subduing task to her childhood had been
    given,
To smooth a darling mother's path through suffering to
    heaven.
And she had found a kindred heart, well worthy of her
    love ;
His mother, too, was gone to join the seraph-band above,
And he had been her darling son, and sweet lessons she
    had given,
To fit for honoured life on earth, and train his mind for
    heaven.
Free from the follies that beset youth's inexperienced
    feet ;
Noble, and frank, and courteous, with accents silvery
    sweet ;
Young Ellis Stamford's youthful days gave promise
    bright and fair,
Of the happy honoured life that had been his mother's
    prayer.
And now a new and holy light had dawned within his
    heart,
Since Annie's lovely image of its visions formed a part;
Brightly, yet oh! too briefly, did the moments glide away
Of that bright and happy morning of life's dark and
    gloomy day.

A sister friend had Annie, but with mind unlike her
    own ;
A winning fair exterior concealed a heart of stone.
Her vows had long been plighted in affection's sacred
    name,
But pride, not love, within her heart had lit a transient
    flame.
Annie had told her all her tale of promised happiness.
She, too, admired young Ellis, and she envied Annie's
    bliss ;
With her, to wish was to achieve—unprincipled and
    vain,
She shrunk not from an action that would give another
    pain ;
With wicked machinations and cruel art she strove
To sow the seeds of dark distrust, and blight the flowers
    of love,—
With persevering efforts, and deep designing skill,
She caused dark doubts of Annie's truth her lover's
    heart to fill.
She hoped that, were he weaned from her, *she* might his
    notice gain,—
The thought of her own perjured vows ne'er woke one
    moment's pain.
Her schemes, so darkly, deeply laid, succeeded but too
    well—
The cruel shock upon his heart with withering influence
    fell.
He lost his faith in Annie, and in all the world beside ;
He madly rushed from home and friends, his crushing
    grief to hide ;—

He took a soldier's coat and sword, and joined a gallant
    band ;
And, spirit-stricken and forlorn, sought a far distant land.
Nor word, nor token, left he, why his heart was thus
    estranged ;
Poor Annie, wondering, waited long, ere she believed
    him changed :
But still he came not—still he wrote not—and his name
    at last,
In hearts that loved him, mingled with fond memories
    of the past ;
And Annie left the scenes of her early joy and grief,
And in Heaven-sent, Heaven-blest duty, soon found a
    sweet relief ;—
The chastening of God's loved ones fell on a heart re-
    signed,
She filled an honoured, useful sphere, by Providence
    assigned ;
The dark, mysterious past, she sought not vainly to
    explore ;
But strove the balm that healed her grief on others'
    hearts to pour.
A loving wife, and tender, happy mother, now become ;
For many years her lovely life shed sunlight o'er her
    home ;
And then they laid her down to rest beneath the grassy
    mound,
And Affection's hand with deathless flowers her precious
    memory crowned.
Years swiftly sped, and Ellis once more trod his native
    shore ;

He found not all that he had left. His father was no
    more.
His dying lips had breathed a prayer for his belovèd
    son,—
A dying blessing was bequeathed to the lost wandering
    one.
He found not all that he had left.—He looked for one
    in vain ;
Oh ! could he but have still believed her fickle, false,
    and vain :
But the cruel truth too soon appeared, how, blinded and
    deceived,
Slanders unfounded and untrue he foolishly believed.
He heard how she had lived and loved, and gone to her
    bright home ;
He watered with repentant tears her lowly, grassy tomb ;
He prayed for faith and love like hers his heavenward
    steps to guide,
That he might meet his Annie there amongst the glori-
    fied.

ON FANCY.

OH! there are currents in the human soul
 That bear it with resistless force away,
Beyond the power of reason's sage control,
 Beyond reality's unbending sway—
And launch it in bright scenes lit up by
  fancy's ray.

The heart, whose inner life is locked and sealed,
 Whose stern surroundings check its outward flow;
Whose hidden depths, unfathomed, unrevealed,
 Hide yearnings for a bliss it ne'er may know—
Some hallowed, peaceful spot where love's bright flowers
  may grow.

Seasons there are when such a heart, inspired
 By sweet imaginings, can plume its wings;
And soaring free, unfettered, and untired,
 'Midst sweet congenial dreams of happy things,
Drink pure rich draughts of bliss from hope's out-gush-
  ing springs.

And check not rudely fancy's daring flight,
　These aspirations of ethereal birth ;
Nor deem their influence shall unfit us quite,
　To listen to the duty-calls of earth—
They cheer and nerve the heart to deeds of truest worth.

And though the dreams most fondly, dearly prized,
　Fade in the light of reason's lamp away ;
Though earth may ne'er behold them realized—
　Earth is not all : there is a brighter day,
Whose glory passeth all e'en fancy can portray.

HEART ECHOES.

HERE is a language of the heart,
    Too deep for speech ;
  Which grammar's rules, and logic's art
    Can never reach.

No ear may trace its mystic tone,
    Yet full and clear ;
It whispers to the heart alone,
    And *that* can hear.

Mysterious, subtile, undefined
    As human thought ;
And often wayward, unconfined
    By human " ought."

All unrestrained by sense and sight,
    Or scenes adverse,
Spirits may mingle and unite,
    And souls converse.

Thus do the mother and her child,
   Ere speech has birth,
Talk of a love, pure, undefiled,
   Strongest on earth.

When standing round the sufferer's bed,
   The lips are sealed,
This hidden language may be read
   In love revealed.

The tongue may say a hundred things
   The heart ne'er knew ;
These echoes from its trembling strings
   Are ever true.

Ne'er let unhallowed passions sound
   These wondrous chords,
Spreading a secret discord round,
   Mightier than words.

Still let us keep faith, hope, and love,
   Threefold, unbroken ;
Our influence then shall heavenward move,
   Though all unspoken.

RETROSPECT AND HOPE.

TOLL! toll!—mournfully, sadly,
    The deep midnight bell for the dying
       year.
  Ring! ring!—joyfully, gladfully,
    Loud peals of welcome—another is here!

Mournfully muse we o'er moments of sorrow,
  Hopes fondly cherished now withered and dead :
Joyfully hail we the coming to-morrow—
  Others more bright may arise in their stead.

Mournfully too doth fond memory linger
  O'er joy-lit hours too rapidly flown ;
But Hope, pointing forward with beckoning finger,
  Still whispers of bliss in the future unknown.

And mournfully too is this solemn hour bringing
  Sad thoughts of the loved and the lost in the tomb :
But onward fleet years, their untiring flight winging,
  Are bearing us home, where no partings may come.

Then farewell, Old Year ! though thy mission is ended,
  Deep lessons of wisdom thy changes have taught ;
By blessings unnumbered our pathway attended,
  Our God we adore for the gifts thou hast brought.

And welcome ! untried one, with all thou art bearing
  Of gloom or of gladness, to sadden or cheer ;
We 'll with firm trust in Heaven, undoubting, unfearing.
  Hope and wish for each other A Happy New Year.

TO HIS ROYAL HIGHNESS PRINCE ALFRED
ON VISITING LIVERPOOL.

THRICE welcome! noble Alfred!
A thousand voices cry;
Thrice welcome! noble Alfred!
A thousand hearts reply.
Music is floating round thee
And the merry bells ring out;
But the sound of truest welcome
Is the honest English shout.
Dear to each true-born Briton,
Our sailor Prince thou art;
And the welcome that we give thee
Is the homage of the heart.

For the sake of thy fond Mother,
Our loved and gracious Queen,
Who through many an hour of peril
Our star of hope hath been—
Whose life hath been a model
Of the gentle, good, and true,—

Who hath decked our England's diadem
  With grace and lustre new ;
In loyalty to her,
  As in heartfelt love to thee,
Banner and bell, and voice and heart,
  Conspire to welcome thee.

And there is yet another,
  Gone hence—but unforgot ;
Whilst goodness is remembered
  His name shall perish not.
ALBERT THE GOOD shall die not,
  In England's proudest story
His name shall add a lustre
  To her greatness and her glory.
Oh ! emulate *his* virtues ;
  Oh ! seek to win *his* fame ;
So England with her Albert's
  Shall couple Alfred's name.

And not alone for others,
  But for thine own dear sake,
These sounds of joy and welcome
  The summer stillness break ;
Young, noble, brave, accomplished,
  Thy bright, untainted name
May grace thy country's annals
  Like another Alfred's fame.

I.

Though thou mayst not sway his sceptre,
   Though thou mayst not wear his crown,
Oh ! may like virtues win for thee
   His deathless, pure renown.

TO MONA.

RIGHT Isle of the Western sea,
    Lit up by the sunset gleam ;
In ocean's arms reclining,
    Peaceful as infant's dream :

With thy mountains of towering splendour,
    Thy valleys of lovely green—
A picture of living beauty,
    Encircled in crystal sheen :

Thoughts of the past cling round thee,
    The scenes of ages gone,
When heroes of ancient story
    Contested thy island throne :

When thy sleeping vales were startled,
    By cannon's echoing roar ;
And the fleets of the fierce invaders
    Brought death to thy peaceful shore.

Gone are those days of carnage,
  Those warriors sleep 'neath the sod ;
And the fields smile in verdant beauty,
  Once stained with the tide of blood.

And of fairies and gentle spirits,
  Whose legends around thee twine,
But few of the best and the brightest,
  Sweet Mona ! remain ever thine.

The spirit of beauty yet lingers,
  In this her beloved retreat ;
And decks with her fairy fingers
  Thy bowers with enchantments sweet.

And the spirit of health still wanders
  By grove, and dell, and shore ;
Blessing the sick and weary
  With vigour and bloom once more.

And the spirit of music is hovering
  O'er many a fairy nook ;
Blending the song of the wild bird
  And the murmur of gentle brook.

And the spirit of poesy dwelleth
  Thy rural charms among ;
Tuning the chords of the bosom,
  And sweeping them into song.

And the spirit of true devotion,
   In many a happy cot,
Kindles, with Heaven-lit radiance,
   Love's light in the hallowed spot.

Hail to thee ! wave-washed Mona !
   Bright gem of the Western sea ;
Long shall bright memories mingle
   Sweet thoughts of delight and thee.

SEA-SIDE THOUGHTS.

MIGHTY, majestic sea! bursting first upon the
    view
  Of the wondering one, to whom thine ever-
    varying charms are new;
  Whose imaginings have vainly pictured what
    the sight would be—
How grandly overwhelming when the eye first rests on
    thee!

Thou ever-changing sea! now reflecting sunny skies,
In undulating ripples thy glad wavelets sink and rise;
But anon an angry conflict with the spirit of the storm,
To fierce, death-laden billows those peaceful waves
    transform.

Thou deep unfathomed sea! what rich treasures are
    concealed!
What dark mysterious secrets in thy depths lie unre-
    vealed!
In vain may human hand essay to bring them forth to
    light,
Thou holdest them securely in thy majesty and might.

Thou heart-dividing sea! bearing loved ones far away;
For whom we vainly yearn through many a long and
    weary day;
Oh! what mournful feelings swell the breast, as we
    muse upon thy shore,
On the friends so far and long away, whom we may see
    no more.

Thou pure and crystal sea! in the better land above,
That land where centres all of beauty, harmony, and
    love,
No tempest darkens o'er thee to disturb thy placid
    breast;
Oh! may we lave in thy bright wave, and be for ever
    blest.

ON THE DEATH OF W. R.

YES ! lay him to his rest ! the man of God,
  Whose feet so long earth's pilgrimage have
    trod ;
  Wearied at length he sinks in slumbers
    blest,
  Lay him and leave him in his peaceful rest.

Yes, lay him down to rest ; his work is done,
Midst cloudless splendour sank his setting sun ;
His name undying fragrance leaves behind :
Long shall it live in many a heart enshrined.

Yes, lay him down to rest ; all that is dust
To the safe keeping of the grave entrust.
He cannot die ; his spirit soars above ;
His memory lingers here embalmed in love.

Lay him to his long rest, nor hopeless mourn
For worth and virtue that may ne'er return ;
Let all who knew him seek with earnest care
To tread his steps, and his rewards to share.

TO MARY.

HOW shall we give thee up?
  Dear to each heart!
How bear the cruel stroke
  Bidding us part?
  Fond Nature fain would say
Stay! thou beloved one! stay!
Hasten not thus away,
  Do not depart.

Why did thine opening charms
  Round our hearts twine?
Why did thy life's bright ray
  Round our steps shine?
Why with such grace arrayed,
Thus bloom, so soon to fade,
Ere years of chilling shade,
  Dearest! were thine.

Vainly we seek to scan
  Things unrevealed.
God's dealings like a scroll
  Secret and sealed,
Check our attempts to pry
Into the hidden "*why*"—
Mysteries from mortal eye
  Wisely withheld.

Loved one! thou seest now
  Clearer than we ;
Heaven's unclouded light
  Shineth round thee.
We saw its rays illume
Thy pathway to the tomb,
Luring thy spirit home,
  From earth set free.

And shall one murmuring thought
  Dare to arraign
His wisdom,—who hath lent,
  And called again ?
Lent to show forth His praise—
Lent to proclaim His grace—
Called to His loved embrace—
  With Him to reign.

Soon to our bleeding hearts
  All shall be clear ;
As we look heavenward,
  Light shall appear,—

Light streaming on the road
Leading to thine abode :
Till then we trust our God ;—
   He cannot err.

BIRDS.

RIGHT, happy birds ! what sorrow have ye ?
From twig to twig, and from tree to tree,
Ever your merry, wild flight winging,
Ever your rapturous wild song singing.

Free as the air through which ye roam,
Fearlessly build ye your tree-top home ;
Rocked by the winds, and fanned by the breeze—
Lulled by the zephyrs that kiss the trees.

Never a dark-boding thought for the morrow
Your glad warbling checketh, or wakeneth sorrow ;
Ye hoard not in barn nor in storehouse your bread,
Of God unforgotten, by Him ye are fed.

Birds ! joyous birds ! were your happy lot mine,
With you would I roam where unclouded suns shine,
To drink of heaven's nectar, and bask in heaven's light,
And flutter and carol in gladsome delight.

Fond mortal ! and wouldst thou thy bright hopes forego
To flutter away a bird's lifetime below ?
If thine more of sorrow, yet thine more of joy,
Eternity's bliss, which death cannot destroy.

"THOU SHALT LOVE THY NEIGHBOUR AS THYSELF."

WEET and pleasant is the duty,
    When the young, the bright, the fair,
In their wealth of winning beauty,
    Ask of our fond love a share

Pleasant as the spirit basking
    In the beams of love-lit eyes ;
To return what they are asking—
    Gushing love's sweet sympathies.

Sweet to love when love is breathing
    Words unutterably kind ;
When affection's hand is wreathing
    Flowery chains the heart to bind.

But more deep and rich revealing
    Lies within this high behest ;

And a nobler, purer feeling,
　　Animates the heaven-taught breast.

Let *thy* love be freely given,
　　Blessing all, unasked, unsought ;
Like the precious dews of heaven,
　　Give it—let it ne'er be bought.

Love the child : but love not only
　　Those already rich in love ;
Seek the wandering, outcast, lonely,—
　　Tell them of a home above.

Let thy love cheer human bosoms,
　　That have yearned for love in vain ;
Where affection's tender blossoms,
　　Blighted, withered, long have lain.

Love the erring,—dark and dreary
　　Shades across their pathway lie ;
Seek to lead the spirit weary
　　To a hope beyond the sky.

Is there one who, malice goaded,
　　Would have worked thee deadly wrong ?
In whose dark thoughts hatred brooded,
　　Filled his bosom—fired his tongue ?

Hate not thou the heart estranged,
    Love him—only seek his good ;
Thy whole soul, transformed and changed,
    Shall reflect the smile of God.

INTEMPERANCE.

INTEMPERANCE ! accursèd fiend !
   Thou hydra-headed monster, hence !
   God grant our households may be screened
   From thy debasing influence.

Destroyer of a nation's peace,
   Foul blot upon a nation's fame ;
When shall thy hated triumphs cease,
   Eclipsed in everlasting shame ?

How many bleeding, broken hearts
   Are crushed beneath thy ponderous heel !
Whilst drop by drop the life-blood starts
   From wounds which none may probe or heal.

How dark thy tale of blasted joys,
   Of proud, fond hopes for ever flown !
Woe's darkest scene thine eye enjoys ;
   Thine ear, the bursting, wringing groan.

Yet come it will, the bright, blest day,
   When England, weary, stricken, sore,
Shall cast thy galling chain away,
   And wear thy cursèd badge no more.

O Thou to whom ten thousand prayers
   (Of hope, save in Thy mercy, shorn)
The midnight on its dark wing bears
   From bosoms stricken and forlorn :

Increase and bless the noble band
   Sworn to resist the hideous foe ;
And grant that soon our much-loved land
   Freedom and happiness may know.

A BIRTHDAY WISH TO A FRIEND

CCEPT on this, thy natal day,
    The wishes of a friend :
Upon thy head in copious showers,
    May Heaven's best gifts descend.

I do not ask thee earthly wealth,
    Or wish thee stores of gold ;
Thy God knows wisely to bestow,
    Or wisely to withhold.

I pray that thou mayst have that pearl
    Which all earth's gems outshines,
Of greater worth than jewels rare
    In rich Golconda's mines.

I dare not wish thee freedom
    From the cares and toils of life,
From sorrows and temptations,
    And the Christian's daily strife.

But I pray that these may lead thee
    To an Everlasting Friend,
That thou mayst in every conflict
    On Almighty strength depend.

Swiftly the years succeeding, bear
    Thee onward to thine home ;
Steady and steadier may thy gaze
    Be fixed beyond the tomb.

A crown, a palm, a sceptre,—
    The song of victory ;
This is, dear friend, the glowing wish,
    My heart now breathes for thee.

AT SEA.

PLASHING and dashing, and ceaselessly
bounding,
  Chasing each other in wild sport away;
Watch we the bright waves our vessel sur-
rounding,
  Roused by the winds into frolicsome play.

Rising in majesty, see! they are nearing,
  Gathering their force as on mischief intent;
But onward the proud bark is gaily careering,
  And in feathery spray all their threatenings are
spent.

See! on their bosom the glad birds of ocean
  Gracefully rest from their wild soaring flight;
Gliding serene 'midst the tossing commotion,
  Over the billows like spirits of light.

Land hath its charms, with its valleys and mountains;
  But oh! there are sweeter attractions for me
Than in rose-perfumed bowers or pure silvery fountains,
  In the tossing—the dashing—the foam-crested sea.

MY FATHER'S BIRTHDAY.

HOW shall I tell thee, father,
    The thronging thoughts that rise,
Winging my fervent prayers
    To Him who rules the skies?

Thoughts of the past come o'er me;
    Again I seem to be,
A little prattling infant
    Beside my father's knee.

Once more I fondly listen
    To words of holy truth,
Lessons of sacred wisdom
    To guide my wayward youth.

Once more with loved ones bending,
    In unforgotten tones,
I hear thy prayers ascending
    For thy dear cherished ones.

I thank the God who gave thee
  To bless thy children here;
I thank Him who hath spared thee
  Through yet another year.

May this year be thy happiest,
  May thy life long be spared;
And be an everlasting crown
  Thy fadeless, bright reward.

TO AN EARLY PRIMROSE.

BEAUTIFUL nursling of early spring !
From thy long sleep awakening ;
Lifting thy delicate head towards the sky,
Reflecting its smile on the passers-by ;
Joyfully hail we thy happy birth,
Like stars in the sky ye spangle the earth,
Wordless, yet eloquent whispers ye bring,
Of the beauty and glory of coming spring.
Yet short-lived thy bloom, oh ! lovely flower,
Passing away in one brief hour ;
The beauty that charmed the eye is fled,
Thou art plucked from thy humble grassy bed,
And we mourn thy death as we hailed thy birth—
Such are the fleeting joys of earth.

TO THE MOON.

CALMLY sitting in lonely splendour,
   On the throne of night,
Wakening feelings hallowed and tender,
   By thy silvery light.

After the cares and toils that oppress us,
   Through the busy day,
Holier musings arise to bless us,
   Wakened by thy sweet ray.

Many a charm of our childhood has faded,
   Touched by reality's hand ;
Sweetly still o'er the spirit jaded
   Waves thy enchanting wand.

Still shine on in thy peerless beauty,
   Queen of the silent night ;
Teach me to shed o'er life's path of duty,
   Borrowed, celestial light.

TWILIGHT.

HOW sweet is the still, calm twilight,
    When the hum of the day is dying ;
And around us, like spirit voices,
    The gentle winds are sighing.
When the perfume of blossom and flower
    The fragrant air is filling ;
And the influence of the hour
    The troubled breast is stilling.
One by one are the stars appearing
    In the azure arch of heaven,
With sparkling beauty cheering
    The deepening shades of even.
Like truest friends, they are hidden
    When sunshine beams around us ;
Like them, they appear unbidden
    When gloomy shades surround us.
Whilst swiftly around us closing,
    The solemn night-shades gather,
The earth sinks to sweet reposing
    In care of the One Great Father.

He slumbereth not, nor sleepeth—
  His Providence watcheth surely,
And those whom He kindly keepeth
  Rest trustingly and securely.

"I WILL LEAD THE BLIND BY A WAY THAT THEY KNOW NOT."

PLEASANT, happy way, for the little tender
feet,
Where Life's brightest sunbeams play, and
earth's opening beauties meet;
And the wondering little thoughts to unfolding bliss expand,
And the little steps are guided by an unseen Saviour's
hand.

Dangerous, slippery way for the unshod foot of youth,
Where error's mists are hiding the beacon light of truth;
Where snares and pitfalls lurk for unwary pilgrims
spread,
Safe and happy only they by that unseen Hand still led.

And onward still and upward through many a steep
ascent,
When childhood's joy has faded, and youth's first
strength is spent,

And the spirit shrinks from conflict with the stern de-
    mands of life,
Courage ! press on ! that unseen Hand shall aid thee in
    the strife !

And narrower, thornier still, seems the way, and darker
    grown,
For earthly love-lights from the sky, are fading one by
    one ;
And sorrow's tempest gathers round, filling the soul
    with dread.
Fear not ! e'en through the darkness thou art safely,
    wisely led.

And onward ! still untiring, when darkness yields to
    light,
And bowers of rosy pleasure to rest and ease invite,
Less dangerous is the conflict than sloth's inglorious
    bed,
Still onward by that guiding Hand thy faltering steps
    are led.

Pause not to seek the hidden cause, why in this vale of
    tears,
Still o'er Life's journey hangs the cloud of cares, and
    griefs, and fears.
Press forward ! once arrived at home, the blaze of
    heavenly light
Shall cause thy wondering heart to own thy Saviour led
    thee right.

A BOAT SONG.

ONCE more on the yielding wave,
   For a tranquil hour afloat ;
And the gentle billows lave
   The sides of our tiny boat.

Away ! with a free, glad bound,
   She clears the receding shore,
With the soothing measured sound
   Of the splash of the dipping oar.

Like a sea-bird, on she hies,
   And the glad waves, sparkling bright,
Reflect the unclouded skies
   In diamond flashes of light.

Onward ! away and away,
   Pull we our little boat ;
Leave we the sheltering bay,
   On the dancing sea to float.

Now the receding day
   Goes out at the doors of the west;
And the bright moon's rising ray
   Silvers the ocean's breast.

And our peaceful evening song,
   In which hearts and lips rejoice,
Is borne by the winds along,
   With the murmuring wave's sweet voice.

Now landward our bark again
   Hies to the stroke of the oar;
And hushed is our evening strain,
   As we spring to land once more.

TO A FRIEND.

ESUS protect thee !   His Spirit defend thee—
   His Word be thy light—thy direction—
     thy guide !
   Angels watch o'er thee.   On high they
     await thee ;
Press to thy Home, for thy Saviour hath died !

Murmur not—loiter not—onward, untiring,
   Though dangers and darkness around thee are spread ;
Light is vouchsafed thee, whilst trustingly seeking
   Wisdom and guidance from Jesus, thine Head.

More than thine enemies, though they are mighty,
   Are the sweet, soul-cheering promises given ;
Suffer thy faith not a moment to waver :
   Conquering—triumphant—'twill bear thee to Heaven.

"IT IS I; BE NOT AFRAID."

WHEN my feet grow tired and weary
    With the long and toilsome way;
When the sky lowers dark and dreary,
    As the sunlight fades away;
    When hope's promise-bloom of gladness,
Withers 'neath affliction's shade;
Saviour! whisper 'midst my sadness
    " It is I ; be not afraid."

When the howling tempest round me,
    Hourly darker, wilder grows,
And the angry waves surround me,
    Threatening o'er my head to close ;
As the unequal conflict waging,
    May my spirit, filled with dread,
Hear, above the tempest's raging,
    " It is I ; be not afraid."

When death's cold and icy finger
    Touches life's fast failing springs ;

And my spirit fain would linger
  ’Midst the old familiar things ;
May the heavenly day-spring breaking,
  Pierce the dark and solemn shade ;
Saviour may I hear Thee speaking—
  “ It is I ; be not afraid.”

When in “ majesty transcendent,”
  Seated on Thy great white throne,
With Heaven’s countless hosts attendant,
  Thou shalt come Thy saints to own ;
By Thy death’s atoning merit—
  By the ransom Thou hast paid—
Sweetly re-assure my spirit—
  “ It is I ; be not afraid.”

A COMMUNION HYMN.

UMBLY coming to Thy table,
    Rendered by Thy mercy able
    Thus to join Thy family,
    In remembrance, Lord, of Thee.

Now the precious life-bread breaking,
Now the sacred emblems taking
Of Thy passion on the tree,
In remembrance, Lord, of Thee.

Of all help save Thine despairing,
Thy sweet invitation hearing ;
I am come Thy guest to be,
In remembrance, Lord, of Thee.

Trusting not in my own merit,
May thy promised, blessed Spirit,
Fill with peace and purity,
As I here remember Thee.

And when Love's great work completed,
On Thy throne of glory seated,
Thou shalt come my Judge to be,
Jesus ! then, remember me.

A FLY'S SECRET.

ACH dear little friend
    I beg to attend
To this short, simple tale of a fly ;
    And though 'tis but a fable,
    I think they 'll be able
Instruction to gain, if they try.

    By a bright summer day
    Invited to stray,
I joyfully buzzed to and fro,
    Till I lit on a curl
    Of a fair, bright-haired girl,
With her a short distance to go.

    Arrived at her home,
    She entered a room
Where her mother with visitors sat ;
    All stylish and gay,
    They had called that fine day
For a few minutes' sociable chat.

" Dear Madam !" each cries,
With affected surprise,
" How lovely your daughter has grown !
How graceful her air !
Her complexion how fair !
What bliss such a darling to own !"

Thus praised and admired,
With flattery inspired,
Young Miss proudly drew up her head ;
When they rose up to go,
I felt curious to know
If they really had meant what they said.

So, fluttering around,
I speedily found
A flower on a bonnet so gay ;
And in that snug retreat
As we passed down the street,
I heard one of the dear creatures say :—

" What a pert, forward puss !
What a terrible fuss
Her mother does make, to be sure !"
Cried the other—" Just so ;
I for one, as you know,
Such vanity cannot endure."

What a pity, thinks I,
That e'en a small fly
Should witness such heartless deceit !

So in hopes it may warn
All it may concern,
I have told what I heard in the street.

Little Misses, I pray,
Ne'er believe all they say,
Who your beauty and loveliness praise;
Rest assured, no *true* friend
To such flattery would bend,
Or seek foolish fancies to raise.

THE SLEEPER AWAKENED.

SLEEPER! on the raging billow
    Rocked in danger's arms to rest;
Rouse thee from the enchanted pillow,
    Shake the stupor from thy breast.
    Here Jehovah's power is round thee—
Here His judgments are abroad;
Break the fetters that have bound thee!
Wake! and call upon thy God!

Sleeper! dreaming in thy slumbers
    Of some new, unreal heaven;
Whilst in magnitude and numbers
    Swell thy sins all unforgiven.
Mercy, that would now entreat thee,
    Soon shall seal thy righteous doom.
Rouse thee! ere the tempest meet thee,
    To the ark of safety come.

Sleeper! in life's vineyard wasting
  Precious, golden hours away;
Whilst thy sun is swiftly hasting
  To the closing hour of day.
Hear thy Master's voice requiring
  Reckoning for the talents given!
Wake! and watch! and work untiring!
  Toil shall sweeten rest in heaven.

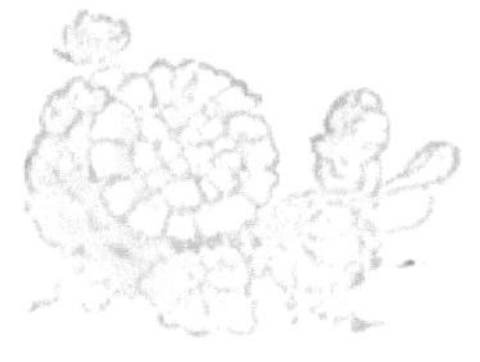

"BEGINNING AT JERUSALEM."

Luke xxiv. 47.

EGINNING at Jerusalem! that heaven-honoured place,
  That spot so dear and sacred to Judea's favoured race;
  There—where within their garnished tombs the martyred prophets slept,
The city o'er whose coming doom, the loving Saviour wept.

Beginning at Jerusalem! where He Himself had taught;
Wherein His wondrous heaven-attesting miracles were wrought,
Where listening crowds had oft been held by a resistless spell,
To hear the truths that from His lips in heavenly accents fell.

Beginning at Jerusalem! which crucified "the Good,"
Where yelling, maddened multitudes had clamoured for His blood,

Where scribe, and priest, and elder had led the bitter
    cry,
" His blood be on us and our sons! but let this Jesus
    die !"

Beginning at Jerusalem ! oh, depths of love and grace !
That mercy should be offered first to that rebellious
    place ;
Sure no poor trembler hence may doubt His saving
    power to prove,
Since e'en His bitterest enemies and murderers shared
    His love.

Beginning at Jerusalem ! and mighty unction came,
And wondrous inspiration, and cloven tongues of flame,
For the promise of the Father in that hallowed spot
    came down,
And three thousand happy witnesses stood up their Lord
    to own.

Beginning at Jerusalem ! oh ! let the tidings roll,
The glad waves of salvation o'er our world from pole to
    pole,
Till all mankind shall be through Christ accepted and
    forgiven,
And our regenerated earth become a second heaven.

AFTER A NIGHT OF THUNDER AND LIGHTNING.

ELCOME, morning! for the night hath been
One of terror, whilst the lightning's sheen
Made the air ablaze with living light—
And the pealing thunders startled night:
Heaven's grand artillery, but held in sway
And made to serve His purposes, whose way
Is in the whirlwind, and whose holy will
E'en clouds, and storms, and tempests must fulfil.
So shall morning break upon the scene
More grand than heart conceives, or eye hath seen,
When the last thunders rend earth's trembling frame,
And the last lightnings wrap it up in flame;
When all that now pollutes is swept away,
And earth regenerated springs to day,
Free from the curse—from death and woe—and sin—
What joy shall hail that glorious morning in!
But where! oh, where shall be the sinners then?
The Heaven defying—God forgetting men?

Who scorn His precepts—slight His proffered grace,
And, save in danger, never seek His face?
Nor rocks, nor mountains, in that hour of dread,
Shall screen the wretched sinner's guilty head.
My Saviour! now as then be Thou my guide,
Then safe 'midst nature's wreck shall I in Thee con-
 fide!

TO E—— ON HER BIRTHDAY.

 SUPPOSE it's your birthday sometime now
about,
But as to just *when* I believe there's a doubt;
But though we mayn't know to a day quite
exact,
No doubt you *are* born; that at least *is* a fact.

And many returns of the day may you see,
And happy ones too, whichever it be;
But happiness follows on goodness, you know,
So better and happier both may you grow.

But remember, dear girl, there's a heavenly birth,
As taught by our Saviour when here upon earth,
May this be your portion,—renewed by His love,—
Old things passed away,—born again from above.

"ONE IS NOT."

"ONE is not!"   There's a vacant seat,
   When the family circle together meet.
   The links of the chain that love had
      wrought
   Are rudely severed, for "One is not."

There's a silent voice in the household song,
There's a missing step in the joyous throng,
There's a smile which the eye in vain hath sought,
There's an aching void, for " One is not."

" One is not."   Thus in days of old
When Joseph was into Egypt sold,
The blood-stained coat to his father brought
Wrung the wild cry, " My son is not."

But, whilst he mourned his Joseph dead,
He, by unerring wisdom led,
From bondage to princely honour brought,
Deliverance for the nations wrought.

o

So, whilst with agonising woe
We mourn o'er the vacant place below ;
A soothing hope to our hearts is given,
That our loved and lost one is safe in heaven.

An added harp in the angel-choir ;
Swelling the deathless anthem higher ;
Another voice in the chorus sweet—
Another crown cast at Jesu's feet.

Another safely entered in,
Beyond the reach of sorrow and sin ;
Soon shall *we* reach that blissful shore
And greet our beloved ones, and part no more.

STANZAS.

 WITHER, O trembling soul,
Dost thou so swiftly speed?
Rapid the days succeed
That bear thee to thy last mysterious
goal.

The spirit's craving hope
Still wanders far and wide,
Restless, unsatisfied,
With earthly pleasure's tantalising cup.

And whilst thine hand would try
To grasp some seeming prize,
E'en in the embrace it dies;
And thou art left to mourn its falsity.

Is this then thy sole fate?
Thy noblest destiny?
Must all these longings die,
These yearnings for a more congenial state?

Why were these visions given
Ne'er to be realised,
Leaving, when highest prized,
The heart they twined around forlorn and riven?

Amidst the gathering gloom
Of reason's darkened ray,
Bright beams of heavenly day
Over my troubled soul seem peacefully to come.

Look through the telescope
Of free and sovereign grace,
Across the unfathomed space
On the bright scene beyond thee for thine hope.

A rest serene and calm,
A joy pure—unalloyed—
Thy every wish supplied
In bliss immortal, full, where nought shall harm.

Ask not a closer view!
Eye may not—cannot see
What is laid up for thee.
Go! serve thy God, and find His promise true!

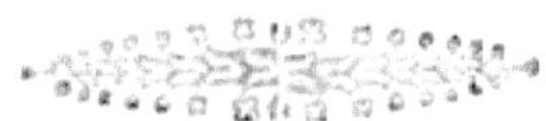

THE FAREWELL OF THE DEPARTING YEAR.

MORTAL! attend! for, ere we part,
    Fain would I commune a while with thy
        heart,
    Start not my solemn appeal to hear,
    Not long may my accents strike thine ear.
Not long may the fleeting moments last,
Ere I am numbered with ages past.

I came in the freshness of Hope's bright bloom,
And welcomes pealed forth from spire and dome.
Say, did no high resolves arise?
Were breathed *no* vows and promises?
As thy heart mused sadly on by-gone years,
What meant those humble and contrite tears?

I go, but oh! by the moments flown,
Whose records are with the Eternal One,

Chain not to earth thy hopes and love,
But treasure them up in the realms above.
I go, but my records shall meet thee again ;
Oh may this hour seal thy happiness then !

ON THE DEATH OF W. S.

APPY spirit, now released
    From thine earthly house of clay,
Lodged in thy Redeemer's breast,
    Circled with eternal day!

Who can tell the wondrous glory
    Of the crown that decks thy brow?
Lit with living, sparkling jewels,
    Souls redeemed from endless woe.

Every prayer-sought, Heaven-blest token
    Of thy labours in the Lord,
In yon heaven, where thou art resting,
    Shall be crowned with vast reward.

CONSTANCY.

EAREST! believe me still true to thee
    Though stern fate our lot should sever,
The faithful heart that beats for thee,
    Shall cherish thine image ever.

Forgive the doubt that would seem to shade
    My visions of coming joy!
For hope's fairest flowers only bloom to fade,
    And a moment earth's bliss may destroy.

Though not like the sturdy, umbrageous oak,
    In proud independent power,
Which hath firmly stood ; while around it broke
    The storm winds of many a wild hour :

Yet, perchance like the ivy, so fragile and weak,
    That clings to the old oak tree,
My spirit may strength and supporting seek
    As it clings to its God and thee.

MUSIC.

GIVE music to the infant,
    In the tender soothing song,
In gently murmuring lullabies,
    From a fond mother's tongue.
    Attune the little heart-chords
To sweet, melodious lays ;
And their echoes shall re-waken
    In future, darker days.

Give music to the happy,
    In youth's bright and hopeful hour,
Across the joyous spirit
    The rapturous numbers pour ;
With skilful hand and ear,
    Or with sweet, melodious voice,
Give expression to the feelings
    That bid the heart rejoice.

Give music to the careworn ;
    At peaceful close of day,

Across the jarring heart-strings
  Let soothing, sweet airs stray.
'Twill cool the spirit's fever,
  'Twill charm the weary breast ;
And sweet dreams shall come to hover
  O'er strength-restoring rest.

Give music to the toiling,
  In the gloomy city room ;
Let tuneful, long-known melodies,
  Like inspiration come,
And dreams of fields and brooklets,
  And of all things bright and fair,
Perchance those sounds may waken
  In the heart oppressed with care.

Give music to the dying,
  When the spark of waning life
Is trembling in its socket,
  And Nature's last dread strife
Shakes spirit, soul, and body,
  With the separating pain ;
Let songs of Jesu's precious love
  The fainting mind sustain.

There is music—sweetest music,
  Ever floating round the Home
To which our loving Father
  Is bidding us to come.

Let it cheer us on our journey,
    Let it tune our hearts to love ;
No jarring string shall enter,
    'Midst the golden harps above.

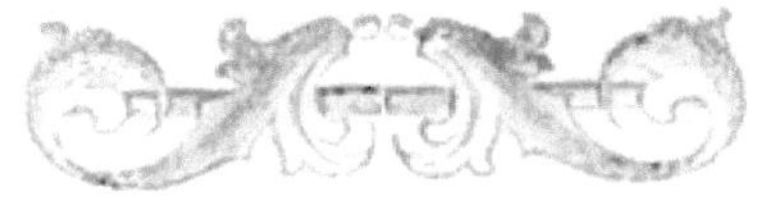

OLD LETTERS.

RECIOUS relics of by-gone years !
Worn with handling, and stained with tears,
Linking the heart with a golden chain
To the days that may never return again.
Mighty your spell and wondrous your power!
'Trancing the spirit for one brief hour,
Bridging the chasm of wasting time—
Wafting us back to a happier clime,
Where birds, and music, and sunshine, and flowers,
Made up the dream of youth's fairy hours.

Gently, carefully, one by one,
Trace we the record of years long flown.
Once more holding communion with those
Now locked in their solemn, long repose.
Many a voice and many a face,
Hushed and stilled in the grave's embrace,
Start from the silence of death once more,
And speak and smile as they did of yore.

And we dry the tear and we check the sigh,
For we feel these heart-links cannot die ;
We know *they* live in a holier sphere,
And with holier love they await us there.

Others there are still left below,
But hid by the mists of long ago.
Fancy pictures what *once* they were,
But vainly guesses what *now* they are.
Time and change have stolen the friend,
And nought remains ours but the lines they penned.

How few remain of the friends of youth !
How doubly precious their time-tried truth !
They too are changed, for their letters bear
Not less of affection, but far more of care.
Index true of the altered face,
Is the altered feeling we here may trace.
Well ! be it so !   Let earth's joys decrease,
Heaven shall unite us in changeless bliss.

THE RETURN OF THE JEWS.

THEY are coming! they are coming! through
the glass of prophecy,
By the light of Inspiration, gathering mul-
titudes I see,
Coming from the distant islands, and from
many a far off strand ;
Coming back to claim their birthright in Judea's hal-
lowed land.
Banished long and scattered widely o'er the spacious
earth abroad,
To succeeding generations witnessing the truth of God.
Scattered into every nation, God's just threatenings to
fulfil,
Kept miraculously separate, God's peculiar people still.

They are coming! they are coming! slowly, brightly
dawns the day,
And the hindrances are rolling like the morn-chased
clouds away ;

Every mountain shall be levelled, and raised valleys
    shall afford
Straight, prepared, and easy pathways for the people of
    the Lord;
For the glory of all nations yet Jerusalem shall
    be,
Unborn thousands yet shall wonder her magnificence
    to see;
For the God of covenant promise round her His pro-
    tection throws;
He shall bless all those who bless her, He shall recom-
    pense her foes.

They are coming! they are coming! from the shades of
    unbelief,
Looking on their piercèd Saviour, filled with peniten-
    tial grief;
For the veil is slowly rolling from proud Judah's heart
    away,
And the Morning-star is beaming with a wonder-work-
    ing ray,
And the latter days' bright glory soon shall flood our
    darkened world,
When the blood-stained flag of Calvary in *their* midst
    shall be unfurled,
When the banished seed of Abraham shall the diadem
    gladly bring,
To the long-rejected Jesus, their Messiah, and their
    King.

They are coming! they are coming! Zion's children
    from afar ;
Nations shall be blessed in her when her glory shall
    appear ;
Blessed sign shall be their gathering to their country
    and their God,
For the full tide of salvation then shall roll our earth
    abroad.
Well may God's believing children hope, and wish, and
    work, and pray
For the promised, long-expected, and now swiftly-
    dawning day,
When the calling in of Israel to the Gentile world shall
    bring
Full revealings of the glory of the Galilean King.

THE SEASONS.

OR the promise sweet Spring bringeth
  Of the rich and verdant year;
For the blossoms that she flingeth
  Sense, and eye, and heart to cheer;
For the soft airs breathing round us,
  For the gems that deck the sod,
For the beauties that surround us—
  Thank and praise the Giver—God.

For the summer painting brightly
  The sweet flowers we love to see;
Whilst around are dancing lightly
  Bird and insect gay and free;
For the golden rays outpouring,
  Filling the rich ears with food,
Ready for the Autumn storing—
  Thank and praise the Giver—God.

For the Autumn with its treasure
  Of the yellow, ripened grain;

Gifts and blessings without measure,
  Sent to cheer the heart of man ;
For the bounties He is spreading
  In the teeming earth abroad,
For the ripe fruits He is shedding—
  Thank and praise the Giver—God.

For the Winter coming surely,
  To renew the wearied ground ;
For the snows descending purely,
  Whitening all the plains around,
Re-invigorating Nature—
  Scattering wholesome frosts abroad,
Magnify the great Creator—
  Thank and praise the Giver—God.

KNOCKING AT THE GATE OF HEAVEN.

LITTLE blue-eyed Katie—little darling Belle,
　　Going home from school to the friends they
　　　　love so well,
　　Going hand in hand with little pattering
　　　　feet,
And little silvery voices holding converse low and sweet.

"Bella, dear," said Katie, "oh where can our Charlie
　　be?
Now don't you wish he'd come again to play with you
　　and me,
And laugh, and skip, and run in the long bright sum-
　　mer day?—
Why did they put him in a box and carry him away?

"Dear mother looked so sad as she stood beside his bed,
And her tears fell down so fast as she told me he was
　　dead;
And yet I think it cannot be a dreadful thing to die,
For she says that now dear Charlie is an angel in the
　　sky.

"She says he has a happy home where all is fair and
    bright,
Where golden streets are thronged with lovely forms of
    shining light ;
That he wears a glittering crown, and the sweetest
    music plays
On a little golden harp, tuned to join the Saviour's
    praise.

" And mother says that Jesus smiles so sweetly on him
    there,
And that from his darling face He has wiped off every
    tear.
Oh ! if we could but go all that happiness to see !
I wonder ! oh, I wonder wherever heaven can be !"

" Oh ! *I* can tell you, Katie," said Bella, with delight ;
" I saw just where they took and laid dear Charlie that
    sad night.
If *that* is heaven, where he is gone, I 'll take you
    straight away.
We 'll go and see that happy place this very, very day."

Then on went little pattering feet, with quick and ear-
    nest tread—
Onward to seek the quiet spot where rest the silent
    dead.
Their footsteps quickened—eyes grew brighter—little
    hearts beat fast,—
As their long and weary walk brought the wished-for
    spot at last.

But oh! it seemed so lonely as they neared the dark
    vault door,
And from the darkening sky heavy drops began to pour,
And Katie's blue eyes filled as she said in tones of fear,
"O Bella! what a dreadful place! I can't see Charlie
    here!"

"I'm sure," said Bella, "he *is* here—dear Katie, don't
    you cry;
I saw them put him in, for ma' and I were standing by.
You know the other side may be very bright and fair;
We'll knock and knock so loud till we make the angels
    hear."

And little hands are knocking at the heavy iron door;
And little trembling voices calling "Charlie" o'er and
    o'er;
But all is still and silent, save the thunder-cloud's wild
    clash—
And the deepening gloom is lit only by the lightning's
    flash.
Till tired and very frightened they sadly leave the place,
And, fast as rain-drops, tears are streaming down each
    little face.

Little clothes wet through with the storm that beat so
    fast,—
Little hearts all sad with dark sorrow overcast,—
Little golden ringlets drooping heavy with the rain,—
Little trembling footsteps sought their homeward path
    again.

"Mother, dear," said Katie, as on that loving breast
Her weary aching head found its own dear place of
    rest,
"We've been knocking at heaven's door, but Charlie
    would not come,
We wanted him to show us his beautiful bright home.

"Do you think that he was far away, playing with
    angels bright?
Or perhaps by now he has forgotten little Katie quite,
And would not know my voice though he heard me at
    the door,"—
And the choking sobs welled up so fast, Katie could say
    no more.

And her mother sweetly told how the body resting lay,
Whilst the spirit soared from earth to bright regions far
    away;
She told her how they too must die ere they could meet
    above,
And how Jesus came to fit us for that home of peace
    and love.

She laid her darling snug and warm in her own little
    bed ;
But the downy pillow brought no ease to Katie's aching
    head.
The tender little plant by the storm was stricken down,
A few brief hours of suffering, and the precious life was
    gone.

As the happy spirit fled, held by earthly chains no
  more,
She did not need to stand and knock at heaven's pearly
  door.
They sorrowfully laid her with Charlie in the tomb,
But with joy the angels bore her to Charlie's better
  home.

TO MY BROTHER.

WE once were three, but Death has been
    Amongst our little number,
And now within the graveyard green
    One sleeps in wakeless slumber.
The streams united in the past,
    Are far asunder driven;
And one hath found the ocean vast—
    Eternity and heaven.

We still are three, Death cannot tear
    The threefold cord asunder;
She whom we mourn as sleeping here
    Now wakes in glory yonder.
The bond that binds each heaven-born soul
    Nor time, nor space can sever;
Triumphant e'en o'er Death's control
    We 'll live and love for ever.

EVELYN : A TALE.

WRITTEN AT AN EARLY AGE.

DARKLY and deeply the night shades fell,
Solemnly sounded the midnight bell,
Forth from the proud castle's loftiest tower,
Telling the flight of the day's last hour.
Not a light was seen, not a sound arose,
Hushed was the castle in calm repose,
Slumber had bound with silken chain
Each heart and eye in that proud domain,
Save one that had left her downy bed,
And wandered forth with noiseless tread ;
Unheard e'en by the watcher's ear
Whose charge was the castle's nightly care.
Beauteous and lovely, a cherished flower,
The pride of her father's lordly bower,
Was she who had left her childhood's home
Through the gloomy forest path to roam.
Again and again that deep bell tolled
The flight of the hours as they onward rolled,

Till the sun with radiance pure and bright
Shed over the landscape a flood of light ;
It glanced upon knights in armour clad,
And maidens whose hearts and eyes were glad,
And the festive morn was ushered in
By the wild notes of mirth and the trumpet's din,
For a bridal party had gathered there,
And lordly knight and maiden fair
Were found in the bridegroom's joyous train,
As he came the hand of his bride to claim.
Noble, and gallant, and brave was he,
The pride of Britain's chivalry.
But in vain had he sought the lady's hand
But for her proud sire's stern command.
Another, her father's foe, had strove
To win the beauteous Evelyn's love ;
In secret his suit had Sir Henry prest,
And his image was lodged in her faithful breast.
He had steered his course for a distant shore,
But had promised, when once his wanderings o'er,
To return amidst glory and wealth and fame
Her loving heart and hand to claim.
She believed and she trusted, and fancy brought
Rich visions of hope to gild each thought
Of one who had wooed but to betray
That heart which as worthless he cast away.
Meanwhile a lord was her father's guest,
And the power of her charms his heart confessed ;
And her sire enforced his stern command
To yield to his prayer her unwilling hand.
But when the fair sun his rays had shed

On the bridal morn—the bride was fled!
In vain the distracted parent sought
Her hiding-place—he found it not ;
And the bridegroom returned to his halls of state
With his proud heart smitten and desolate.
Months rolled and closed that mournful year,
But no tidings met the father's ear
Of his fugitive child, and smitten in grief,
He refused consolation, nor found relief,
And summer again with verdure crowned
Shed radiance and fragrance and beauty around.

PART II.

A fair lady wandered at sunset hour
To a calm retreat, a sylvan bower.
Her maiden, as young and fair as she,
Had won her confidence full and free,
For in her she had found a faithful friend,
The choicest boon Heaven deigns to lend.
'Twas the bridal eve of that lady fair,
And long she lingered whispering there
To her youthful attendant her dreams of bliss,
And visions of future happiness ;
And ere she slept she bid her pray
That blessings might crown the coming day.
The maiden had ne'er beheld the knight
Whose praises were breathed in her ear that nigh
But she uttered a fond and fervent prayer
That he might prove worthy of love so sincere,

That no shade of sorrow or grief might rise
To blight her friend's hopes, or to darken her skies.
That lady's maid was Evelyn fair,
Who sought concealment and shelter there
Till her lover should come from a distant shore,
And her years of trial and waiting be o'er.
Alas! alas! he had long returned,
But not to the heart that for him had spurned
Wealth, rank, and honours.   He sought her not.
Her beauty and love were alike forgot.
His vows to her, so solemnly spoken,
Were heartless and false, and lightly broken,
He basely boasted of triumphs won
Over trusting hearts, and hers was but one
Of the many whose memory now to him
Was no more than a passing, long flown dream.
The morn arose, and the gentle maid
In her bridal robes her lady arrayed.
She had fastened the last luxuriant tress,
And breathed a fond prayer for her happiness,
And marked the soft blush that stole over her cheek
As she passed from her room her lover to seek,
And the deeper that chased that faint blush away
As he gently chided her long delay.
But Evelyn's heart now sunk with despair,
In the bridegroom she sees Sir Henry there.
He inherits another and nobler name,
But each winning accent and smile is the same
That had chained her memory with magic power
Through many a lonely, dreary hour.
But who shall paint the stroke that fell

On the trusting heart that had loved too well ?
Unnoticed she passed through the joyous throng,
From the merry laugh and the minstrel's song.
She sought her father's lonely side,
And prayed his forgiveness ere she died.
But the joy that welcomed his child's return
Died out as that child to her grave was borne,
And ere that summer's flowers had shed their bloom,
He slept by her side in the silent tomb.

THE PRODIGAL'S RETURN.

"I WILL arise!" the prodigal said,
   For here I perish for lack of bread ;
   I will go to my father's house, for there
   The meanest servants have bread to spare.

"I will arise!" for my heart is faint,
None here will list to my sad complaint ;
My summer friends in my darker hours
Have flown to revel 'midst pleasure flowers.

"I will arise!" for false as fair
I have found each bright seductive snare
That lured me from virtue, friends, and home,
In the crooked paths of sin to roam.

"I will arise!" while yet I may,
Ere hope's last spark has died away ;
Whilst yet my weak step may homeward move,
For my heart is fainting for bread—and for love.

"I will arise!" and the deed is done!
Homeward hastens the penitent son ;
Not proudly his portion to demand,
But a humble suppliant there to stand.

Not yet had his eye beheld the dome—
The first faint glimpse of his childhood's home--
When afar he sees—oh! can it be
His injured sire ?   Yes! yes! 'tis he.

Coming swiftly with love-winged haste,
His arms round his desolate boy he cast,
And he stopped the plea for a servant's place
With the pardoning kiss and the fond embrace.

And the robes, and the shoes, and the ring are
        brought,
And his crimes and disgrace are alike forgot ;
And the merry feast is unsparingly spread—
For the son is alive, once mourned as dead!

Saviour ! we thank Thee, whose tender love,
To win us back to our home above,
Hath sweetly taught how the Father yearns
Till each weary, wandering child returns :

How Heaven itself is moved to see
Man's sin-made woe and misery ;
And how sweeter anthems surround the Throne
As the Father receives each returning son.

THE BOY OF HAARLEM.

A touching incident occurred at Haarlem, in Holland. A little boy, about eight years old, the son of a man employed in repairing the dykes, so numerous in that country, had been sent by his mother to carry some provisions to a poor old man living at some distance. On his return, he heard an unusual sound of trickling water, and, on tracing it, found a small hole in the dyke. Fearful that if he left it whilst he went to acquaint his father, it would, in the meantime, burst through the embankment, and expecting some one would be passing, he put his little finger into the hole, which had the desired effect of stopping it. But unfortunately no one came, and the little fellow stood the whole night until four o'clock the next morning, when a doctor, accidentally passing, heard a groan, and found it proceeded from the child. In utter astonishment he inquired what he was doing there: "Keeping the water from running through," was the simple yet noble reply of the little hero, whilst the quivering lip and trembling limbs alone gave token of the intense pain of that long and weary night.

BEHOLD him, as with song and glee
   He revels 'midst the flowers ;
Eight summers scarce have cheered his heart
   With bright and sunny hours.

His joyful steps he homeward bends,
  With his young heart gay and free !
For the poor man's prayer hath lighted there,
  And who so blithe as he ?

The " shades of evening " close around
  As he homeward wends his way,
But the pale moon sheds upon his path
  Her bright and silvery ray.

And now his home he soon had gained,
  But a sound attracts his ear ;
He listens,—and his little heart
  Beats high with anxious fear.

The gates were closed against the flood,
  And aye full well he knew
That dire destruction would ensue
  If the dreadful foe break through.

So carefully he searches round
  Till by the moon's fair beam
The small aperture soon he found,—
  The inlet of the stream.

Well pleased, his little finger serves
  To stem the danger nigh,
Whilst gladness fills his little breast
  And sparkles in his eye.

But night grows deep and deeper still,
    And, as its hours roll on,
Benumbed with cold, that child remains
    At that brave post alone.

Say, did *no* thoughts of home intrude
    Upon his little breast ?—
His pillow—where his wearied head
    Might sink to peaceful rest ?

His friends, to whom his lengthened stay
    Would many a pang impart ?
Yes ! through that long, long night of woe,
    Each flitted through his heart.

But he knew if he left the gap unstopped,
    And the foe should burst its way,
'Twould sweep the home and the friends he loved
    With resistless force away.

So nobly, bravely did he stand
    Throughout the weary night,
Though it seemed as the morn would never rise
    To gladden his longing sight.

Tell me not of the heroes of field and fame,
    Whose valour caused thousands to fall ;
The hero of Holland, the boy of Haarlem,
    Hath a name that shall vie with them all.

HE GIVETH HIS BELOVED SLEEP.

MILING lay a little infant
    Sleeping sweetly, purely ;
  Resting 'neath the Father's vigil
    Peacefully, securely.
  And above its cradle hovered
A spirit form, bright guard to keep ;
Thus that kind and tender Father
    Giveth His beloved sleep.

And the infant reaches manhood,
    But the brow is telling
Many a tale of stern, sad conflict
    In the bosom swelling.
But each morning song is bringing
    Thanks for mercies given,
And each evening hour is winging
    Trusting prayers to heaven.
And still that spirit guard is hovering,
    Commissioned tireless watch to keep ;
Whilst the same kind, loving Father
    Giveth His beloved sleep.

And the journey now is ending,
  And life's last hour hasting ;
And beneath affliction bending
  The frail form is wasting.
But a sunbright ray is gleaming
  O'er the darkening vision,
And the spirit sees the beaming
  Of the light Elysian.
And awhile it leaves the body
  To its slumbers long and deep,
Till rewaked by Him who sweetly
  Giveth His beloved sleep.

ON A BALLOON ASCENT.

GOD speed ye! airy voyagers,
        In your adventurous flight;
    And guide you as ye soar afar
        Beyond our wondering sight.
        As if impatient of the bonds
    The earth-chained soul that bind,
For one brief hour ye rise aloft,
    Leaving your mates behind.
What eager, straining, upturned looks
    A thousand anxious eyes
Are bending towards you, as from earth
    Majestic ye arise!
What acclamations rend the air
    When wonder finds a tongue,
To see you on your skyward course
    Sail gracefully along!
But as ye cleave your bird-like path
    Through trackless space on high,
Faint and yet fainter on your ears
    The echoing murmurs die.

And the astonished throngs around
  That hailed your upward flight,
Are lost amid the great expanse
  That opens to the sight.
Thus eagle spirits that have soared
  Beyond their fellow-men,
In nobler thoughts that aye shall live,
  Inscribed by Wisdom's pen,
Have seen and heard unuttered things
  In their sweet spirit flight;
Whilst meaner gilded toys of earth
  Have faded from their sight.
And thus when from the body free,
  Shall the unfettered soul
Triumphant homeward—heavenward rise
  Beyond the grave's control,
God speed you, airy voyagers!
  And not this hour alone,
But till ye rise to join the throng
  Round the Eternal throne.

FREEDOM.

FREEDOM! inspiring word to honest virtue's
    ear!
    Wherever breathed or heard, most hallowed,
        prized, and dear!
    Kindled by Him who came to make His
people free,—
Lighting with quenchless flame the torch of liberty,—
Nerving the powerless arm to seize fair manhood's
    right,—
Girding the fainting heart with stern, resistless might,—
Treading Oppression down 'midst shouts of victory,—
Lifting the down-trod up, and bidding them go free;
Such are the mighty deeds wrought by thy conquering
    name,
But mightier yet shall glow in thy roll of future fame.

Freedom! unfettering word! Proclaim it far and wide!
Till all shall claim the dower God's righteous laws
    provide.

Go! breathe it to the slave groaning beneath his load,—
Tell him his God-stamped form belongs to none but
    God.
And the "*thing*" *becomes a* MAN, and the life-blood
    dances free
As he stands on God's fair earth in native dignity.
Go! breathe it to the nation, long held in iron sway
By a despotic conqueror, bid to crouch and to obey;
Tell them their chains are broken,—give them again
    their right,
And life-giving beams shall dart from Liberty's blest
    light.

Go! breathe it to the soul chained, fettered in mind and
    thought,
Who cannot be, and speak, and do, as by their conscience
    taught;
Where'er true, virtuous man is found, let him the boon
    receive,
Freedom to think, and speak, and act,—his sacred birth-
    right give.
Go! breathe it to the slave of base passions and desires,
Self-tortured and consumed by unhallowed bosom fires;
Show him the thousand graces that heavenly freedom
    wears,
And perchance her smiles may lure from destructive,
    deadly snares.
And when penitence and faith have loosed sin's galling
    chain,
Win him back to paths of peace and purity again.

Oh ! bright shall be the future of our glad and happy
    world,
When Universal Freedom hath her beauteous flag un-
    furled ;
When man shall look on man as a brother and a friend,
And despotism and tyranny find an inglorious end,
And the freedom of the Gospel its transforming power
    assert
In every happy home and emancipated heart.

CONSOLATION.

TIRED and weary of the twilight,
    Longing for the perfect day,—
    Longing for the coming sunlight,
      Which shall chase these mists away.
      Tired of sin, and care, and sorrow,—
  Tired of creature happiness,
Oh! when shall the bright to-morrow
  Usher in eternal bliss?
For the loveliest flowers are fading
  That have cheered me with their bloom,
And my heart and eyes are shedding
  Tear-drops o'er the silent tomb;
For earth's tenderest ties are breaking,
  And my heart yearns for lost love;
Oh! when shall my soul awaking,
  Find the meeting-place above?
Patience, tired one, vainly fretting
  O'er the common lot of life,
And the mighty hand forgetting,
  That upholds thee in the strife.

What though care, and sin, and sorrow
  Weary heart, and hope, and brain,
From God's promise thou canst borrow
  Power to comfort and sustain.
Whilst thy longing eyes are turning
  Glances towards the better land,
The Great Father knows thy yearning,
  All thy times are in His hand.
Thinkest thou He will forsake thee
  When thy heart is pressed with woe?
Thinkest thou there can o'ertake thee
  Trouble that He may not know?
Not a sparrow helpless falleth
  But He marketh its descent,—
Not a hungry raven calleth,
  But its sustenance is sent.
Everything creation needeth
  Doth his skill and love provide,
All Omniscient wisdom heedeth,
  Let thy soul in Him confide.
Lay and leave thy cares before Him,
  Seek to know and do His will,
For His countless gifts adore Him;
  Loving, wise, and gracious still.
Thus shall faith and resignation
  Kindle heaven in thy breast,
Till, complete thy full salvation,
  Thou shalt with thy Saviour rest.

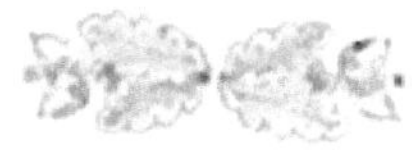

SCENES OF CHILDHOOD.

SCENES of my childhood! as on memory's
        wing,
    I once more wander through each loved
        retreat ;
    And hear with childhood's ear the gay birds
        sing,
And see with childhood's eye the prospect sweet.

How o'er my mind comes rushing back again
    The bright enjoyments of those happier hours !
The richer music of each woodland strain,—
    The lovelier tints that seemed to deck the flowers.

I hear again each old melodious sound,
    Whose echoes still make music in my heart ;
I feel each spell that dancing heart that bound,
    I see,—I hear,—I feel,—and then I start.

From my fond reverie, I start to find
  All changed,—myself,—the birds,—the trees,—
    the skies.
I miss the sound of many an accent kind,—
  I miss the light of tender, loving eyes.

Scenes of my happier years! I love ye still!
  Not over *you*, but *me*, the shadows rest,
That darken the wild beauty of the hill,
  Or dim the charms the lovely vale that drest.

Sweet Darley Dale! with rapture deep and wild
  Thy beauty trances still my heart and eye;
For sure on fairer spot the sun ne'er smiled,
  Nor moon shed glory from the night's clear sky.

And still I love to trace each neighbouring charm,
  The flowery path,—the well-remembered tree;—
The peaceful village, and the smiling farm,
  All fraught with bright remembrances to me.

And thou, dear Winster! nestling tranquilly
  In hill-side cradle; peaceful, happy spot!
Though whispering of the loved and lost to me,
  Thy *living* heart-links ne'er shall be forgot.

There still is power in nature's loveliness
  To breathe into my soul a holy joy,
There still remains full many a well-known face
  Beaming affection from the speaking eye.

Then still I love ye ! scenes to childhood dear.
　Amidst your bright attractions as I rove,
Ye cheer my spirit, as it seeks to steer
　Its sky-ward course to brighter scenes above.

ON THE COMPLETION OF THE ATLANTIC CABLE.

MAJESTIC triumph of the human mind !
    Won by unconquered, persevering skill,
These far Atlantic-severed shores to bind
    With lightning-winged conductors of
        man's will.

When shall his enterprising genius end ?
    To what far heights shall his discoveries soar ?
Where shall his knowledge-craving spirit bend
    And own its want of power to compass more ?

There yet are secrets in the mighty deep,—
    The earth beneath us,—and the air around,
The sky above,—the elements that sleep,—
    The treasures on, or hid beneath, the ground.

Secrets, that only wait men's potent touch
    To break the spell, and flash them forth to day ;
Time's past revealings have unravelled much,—
    What lies hid in the future, who shall say ?

Man's soul, stamped with the print of Deity,
   For glorious immortality designed,
Ever aspires towards infinity,
   Though now awhile by walls of clay confined.

But He who made all things above, below,
   And governs all by laws as just as wise ;
Still condescends to searching man to show
   Each simple, mighty power that latent lies.

All hail the day that sees the proud deed done !
   Completed 'neath approving Heaven's smile ;
The earth's dissevered continents made one
   By the mysterious thought-transmitting coil.

And hail the day that sees the nations own
   The agency and blessing of High Heaven,
And lay the laurels of their triumphs down
   Before His throne, who all success hath given.

And may this mighty space-destroying power
   Hasten the promised swiftly dawning day,
When heavenly truth rich floods of light shall pour,
   And all mankind shall own the Saviour's sway.

QUEEN ESTHER.

SHE stands in her regal dignity,
    The beauteous Jewish queen ;
There is winning loveliness in her face,
    And stateliness in her mien.

But that fair face hides 'neath its sweet sad smile
    A weight of anxious care ;
And scarce may the robe o'er her bosom hide
    The wild heart-throbbings there.

She hath ventured uncalled for, unbidden to stand
    Before her despotic lord ;
And her life depends on the wave of his hand,—
    Her existence upon his word.

For the stern decree hath been issued forth
    Unalteringly severe ;
That in *his* presence, on pain of death,
    Unsummoned might none appear.

And she—the beloved one—for thirty days
  Had never beheld his face ;—
Oh ! will he now to her boldness extend
  The sceptre of kingly grace ?

She hath called each latent beauty up,
  And hath heightened each winning charm ;
And her eye, with affection's pure, bright beam,
  Seeks his proud, stern heart to warm.

But not alone on the power of her charms
  Stays she her fainting hope ;
Prayers for this hour to a Mightier King
  Have been humbly offered up.

And her God hath touched the despot's heart,
  And it melts in tenderness now ;
And the sceptre is reached, and Love's accents ask—
  " Queen Esther, What wilt thou ?"

Oh ! 'twas for *this* that the Jewish maid
  Was decked with beauty rare,
And in Persia's royal robes arrayed
  To stand as a suppliant there.

To work the deliverance of God's race
  From proud Oppression's hand,
And her name in the records of Providence
  Shall ever distinguished stand.

DREAMS.

HEN the life of the day is over,
   And we sink in slumber deep,
They come o'er our couch to hover,
   And kindle new life in sleep.

And faces and scenes long hidden
   By time and by distance from sight,
By their strange, wild influence bidden
   Come again in the silent night.

When reason awhile seems sleeping,
   Busy Fancy seizes the rein,
And anon she is rapidly sweeping
   Our minds through her wide domain.

Were only the world of the *real*
   Intended our thoughts to share,
Oh ! say, would these scenes ideal
   In our sleeping hours appear ?

Come they not life to brighten
   In its dull round of care ?
Come they not hearts to lighten
   Of sorrows that rankle there ?

They come to the sad bereaved one,
   Whose loved ones have passed away,
And again the sweet light of their presence
   Is shedding its wonted ray.

They come where 'midst city shadows
   The child of the country pines ;
And again o'er sweet, flowery meadows
   The gladdening sunbeam shines.

They come where the prisoner's chain
   Clanks harshly and heavily ;
And for one fleeting hour again
   He tastes the sweet joy of the free.

They come where the star of hope
   Hath lost its refulgence bright ;
And the bliss that they conjure up
   Re-kindles its heavenly light.

And sometimes perchance are given
   Stray beams from the world unseen ;
Entrancing visions of heaven,
   With its fields of eternal green.

Granted, these dreams soon perish,
  But which of earth's pleasures remain?
If longer our day-dreams we cherish,
  To lose them gives greater pain.

Though they seem to be vague and unmeaning,
  The flights of a restless brain,
Are they not ofttimes screening
  Revealings of God to man?

Have not truth's pages spoken
  Of many a message bright;—
Many a Heaven-sent token
  In visions of silent night?

As over our slumbers stealing,
  Are they not often fraught
With wondrous and deep revealing
  Of secrets divinely taught?

Let us not proudly scorn them,
  These shapes of the midnight hour,
Let us not weakly adorn them
  With vain Superstition's power.

Those for wise purpose given
  Shall answer the destined end,
Designed by our Father in heaven,
  Whilst we on His love depend.

And when earth's last shadows are breaking.
      Its visions all passing away,
May ours be a blessed awaking
      To the light of eternal day.

TRUE GLORY.

"WHAT," I asked, "is man's highest glory?"
    And my fancy conjured a warrior up;
    And with kindling eye and with stern
        fixed purpose,
    He pointed aloft to his star of hope.
And I saw it gleam through the dense surrounding
Of thick battle clouds that darkened the air;
And I heard the booming cannon sounding,
And shrieks of the dying that mingled there;
But onward he pressed through fields of carnage,
To seize Fame's circlet to deck his brow:
He won it and wore it, a bright, brief season,
But wearer and worn are unheeded now.

And again I asked, "What is *real* glory?"
And the scene was changed, and a statesman sat;
He had craved a proud place in his country's story,
And aspired to be greatest among the great,

And he steadily climbed the dangerous ladder,
And planted his foot on its giddy height :
But scarce had Fame's hand the diadem settled,
When the dark grave hid him from mortal sight ;
And all that remained of the mighty meteor
That had flashed across his country's sky,
Was the shut-up clay in the narrow coffin,
Left alone in dust and decay to lie.

And again I asked, " What then is glory ?"
And the miser looked on his hoards of gold,
And loaded his heavy iron coffers
With shining treasures of wealth untold.
And field to field—and acre to acre—
Gathered he—added he—day by day,
Till Death, the stern creditor, unrelenting
Hurried his earth-bound soul away.
And the fabulous sum of his hoarded treasures
Was squandered and scattered in many a hand ;
Unregretted he fell, and he slumbered forgotten
In his last remaining " six feet of land."

And again the unsatisfied question I uttered,
As I turned from each humbling picture away,—
Oh ! what is the certain path to honour ?
What laurels are those that will never decay ?
And a ray of truth shone pure and radiant,
Where in God's Word the answer beamed,
" Them that honour Me, I will honour,
All that despise Me are lightly esteemed."

And a voice came soothingly over my spirit,
('Twas Wisdom herself that sweetly spoke,)
" Man's highest glory is God's blest service,
His burden is light, and easy His yoke.
There is yet another field of conflict,
Not with mankind, but with error and sin.
There are fadeless honours—enduring treasures—
For the hand of patient faith to win.
Press through opposing spirit legions,
Help on Truth's glorious triumphs below !
Dazzling crowns of eternal brightness
Wait for each overcomer's brow."

LADY JANE GREY.

ILL-FATED Jane ! could no less blow suffice
    Than that which took thy precious life
        away ?
Must thy meek head be the sad sacrifice
    Thy injured country's laws' stern debt to
        pay ?

By pure, unwavering, filial duty taught
    Thy proud, ambitious sire's commands to obey,
Unwilling didst thou quaff the cup he brought
    Of royal honours,—soon to pass away.

Alas ! that loveliness and wisdom, joined
    With rare intelligence, and matchless worth,
And all with heavenly piety combined,
    So soon—so rudely—must be swept from earth.

And as, within thy gentle heart's deep core,
    Stern Justice to the hilt her sword must sheathe,—
Must thou behold *his* corse, besmeared with gore,
    The partner of thy fault, and of thy death ?

Such gifts,—such sorrows, lovely Jane were thine,
  And unborn pitying eyes shall drop the tear
O'er the stern sentence that could thee consign,
  For forced offence, to judgment so severe.

But, as by one fell blow earth's chains were riven,
  Thy uncaged soul to brighter regions fled ;
A crown of glory, by thy Saviour given,
  With fadeless brilliancy adorned thine head.

REMEMBRANCE.

ORGET not the holy dead,
    Whose places are vacant here ;
Resignation herself may shed
    The hallowed, memorial tear.

Our Saviour's humanity wept
    The spoils of the conqueror to see ;
O'er the grave where dead Lazarus slept,
    His tear-drops fell fast and free.

Forget not the mother's love
    That so fondly twined round thee ;
Perchance in her home above
    She still remembers thee.

Nor the father, whose silvery hair
    Gave weight to his counsels wise ;
With affection's tenderest care
    Ever those counsels prize.

Forget not thy sister kind,
    Who sleeps in her wakeless rest ;
Each sweet recollection bind
    To thy fond and faithful breast.

Nor thy brother, when passed away
    From his wonted place on earth ;
Let thy true heart day by day
    Remember his noble worth.

Forget not the darling one,
    Whom death has snatched away ;
The household's sunlight and joy,
    Or the household's prop and stay.

Nor those whose silvery tones
    Made music in home and heart ;
Let the unforgotten ones
    In thy holiest thoughts share a part.

Think of them, not alone
    Sleeping in dark decay ;
Think of their spirits flown
    To realms of eternal day.

Think of them as they reign
    In the palace beyond the sky,
Be their memory a holy chain
    To anchor thine heart on high.

Theirs is the *truest* life,
    'Midst pleasures and joys divine ;
Death's last mysterious strife
    Shall usher thee into thine.

Till then let fond memories sweet
    Cluster within thy breast,
Of those thou shalt once more meet
    In the land of the bright and the blest.

THE HOUSE OF PRAYER.

THERE are noble, towering palaces
    In our dear native land,
Rearing their proud and lofty heads,
    Majestic as they stand.
The marks of rich magnificence,
    And princely wealth they bear,
But nobler to the good man's heart
    Is God's own house of prayer.

There are mansions where the happy
    Are mingling gay and free ;
Where the voice of mirth and the smile of love
    Are blending joyfully.
But sweeter than the joy-beam,
    In Love's circle, bright and fair,
Is the sacred bliss God's presence sheds
    In the holy house of prayer.

They stand the truest ornaments
    Of our dear sea-girt isle ;

Adorned with heavenly beauty,—
With God's approving smile.
Homes of the weary, fainting hearts,
Burdened with sin and care ;
Here they may find restoring strength
In the peaceful house of prayer.

Here songs of heavenly sweetness,
In thrilling notes arise ;
And here ascends the faith-winged prayer
To Him who rules the skies.
And answering showers of grace descend
In rich abundance there.
Oh ! truly, 'tis the gate of heaven—
The hallowed house of prayer.

THE SLAVE.

LOVELY island in the western main,
    Where the new continent extends its shore;
Where beauty holds her undisputed reign,
    And decks with varied charms the land-
        scape o'er.

Three miles in length, by two in breadth it stood,
    Small, yet adorned with many a lovely spot;
With hill and valley, and with field and flood,
    With lordly mansion and sequestered grot.

And birds and insects of rare loveliness
    Flitted from grove to grove,—from tree to tree;
Fit home it seemed for cloudless happiness,
    Shut sweetly in by the encircling sea.

One man, its lord, of noble, generous heart,
    Laws and protection to the island gave;
But here may virtuous indignation start,—
    He held despotic power.   He owned the slave.

But could the monstrous system e'er be fraught
  With benefits or blessings to the race,
Here, surely, was the wondrous secret taught :
  Contentment seemed to smile in every face.

A father he,—a friend to all around,—
  His acts were ruled by motives high and true ;
Rewards the toil of patient labour crowned,
  And kindness sought the stubborn to subdue.

They grew around in many a household band,
  Where Hymen's bonds had hallowed each loved home.
Their willing labour tilled his fertile land ;
  They found no cause, nor felt a wish to roam.

Among the wives and mothers gathered there,
  With the dark skin of Afric's sable race ;
Hannah, adorned with worth and wisdom rare,
  Shone in intelligence and winning grace.

Taught by her partial mistress, not alone
  The duties, but the accomplishments of life ;
Beneath her roof and care had Hannah grown,
  Till she assumed the sacred name of wife.

And not one passing cloud seemed fraught with power
  To cast upon her heart a shade of gloom ;
Save when her thoughts would dwell in lonely hour
  On the far-distant friends of childhood's home.

And now the teeming earth more toil demands,
   And the kind master with a watchful care,
Seeks an addition of assisting hands,
   The labours of his slaves to aid and share.

He pays the price for human flesh and blood,
   Forgive him, Heaven, the foul, unnatural act!
Amidst the bought and sold one negro stood,
   From whom no words nor blows might toil exact.

But lately kidnapped from his native shore,
   He scorned the chain that crushed his liberty:
He scorned to lift his hand to labour more,
   Save in that land which he no more might see.

And now the owner brings his purchase home,
   Trusting that love the stubborn heart would melt;
But scarce to land the vessel's freight has come,
   When with a scream Hannah approached and knelt

Before the slave, whose glances fierce and wild
   Bespoke a mind unconquered still and free;
She knew her father!   He—his long-lost child!
   What joy that father's face again to see!

And now that daughter with affection sought
   To chase his gloomy thoughts and dark despair;
To reconcile him to his altered lot,—
   His lightened yoke of servitude to bear.

He saw around him all that wealth could give,
   Or kindness yield, to soften slavery's lot ;
All that his forced subjection might relieve
   He saw ;—but his proud spirit yielded not.

Day after day he steadily refused
   To do the equal task of toil assigned ;
Day after day his conduct was excused,
   In hopes to win him by forbearance kind.

His daughter's heart with shame and sorrow burned
   To see him on the ground inactive cast ;
To see each kind entreaty coldly spurned,
   As gloomily he brooded o'er the past.

She strained each nerve, not only to supply
   His wants, but lack of service in the field ;
Hoping to see his stern resistance die,
   Hoping to see his stubborn spirit yield.

He saw her toil beyond a woman's strength :
   He knew his miseries caused th' unnatural strain ;
He saw,—and made the dread resolve at length,
   To cast away with life, dark slavery's chain.

One dreadful morn, poor Hannah's wakeful eye
   Beheld her sire with firm and rapid stride,
Reach a tall cliff that reared its proud head nigh,
   And madly dash into the foaming tide !

Wildly she followed.   But, alas ! too late
  She reached the spot, with shortened, wordless breath ;
Too late to snatch him from his dreadful fate :
  She heard him shriek the last wild shriek of death !

The shock unseated reason, and she fled.
  From the poor maniac's now disordered brain
She only sees her darling father dead ;
  She can but hear his drowning cry again.

O slavery ! in thy fairest colours drest ;
  Foul monster ! hideous shape to virtue's eye !
How deep the curses on thy name that rest !
  How doubly deep thy crimes of blood-red dye !

But, as the glory of the latter day
  Illumines the dark places of our world,
Thine every vestige shall be swept away,
  And to oblivion thy dark flag be hurled.

JESSY.

HERE the bright Loddon's waters lave,
    With silvery beauty nigh,
The banks o'er which the tall trees wave
    Beneath the summer sky.

In a sweet spot, which Nature's hand
    Adorned with loveliest bloom,
There dwelt a happy household band
    In their sequestered home.

A widowed mother gathered there
    Her little family,
And trained with fond affection's care
    Her lovely children three.

When England's hand in victory's hour
    Rang Nelson's funeral knell,
With him, beneath the Spaniard's power,
    Their gallant father fell.

The mother, left with slender means,
  But noble and refined,
Sought amidst Nature's loveliest scenes
  To train each opening mind.

And well did time repay her toil,
  As day by day they grew
Beneath indulgent Heaven's smile,
  In health and wisdom too.

Two girls, in every feature fair,
  The mother's charms disclose ;
And one bright boy of beauty rare
  The father's image shows.

Twins were the youngest girl and boy ;
  One, both in soul and heart ;
If one breast swelled with grief or joy,
  The other shared a part.

But now a cloud came o'er their sky,
  Full fraught with bitter woe ;
The light forsook sweet Jessy's eye,
  And sickness laid her low.

In answer to affection's prayer,
  Her health returned once more ;
But, ah ! no medicine, skill, or care
  Her eyesight could restore.

The gentle girl no more might see
  The friends so loved and kind ;
Nor brook, nor bird, nor flower, nor tree ;
  Poor Jessy now was blind.

But William, with redoubled love,
  And sympathising grief,
With tender skill unceasing strove
  To seek and give relief.

He led her to each much-loved spot
  Her happy childhood knew,
And to the sweet sequestered grot
  Where fragrant wild-flowers grew.

On the rude bridge, where, deep beneath,
  The rippling waters flowed,
Railings he put to guard the path
  Where Jessy's footsteps trod.

And thus they passed from year to year
  From childhood into youth !
Each to the other still more dear
  In bonds of love and truth.

But now the time drew near to part
  The bond so firmly tied ;
William must far away depart,
  And seas their lot divide.

An uncle's wishes to fulfil,
  He joined a soldier band ;
Ordered a gallant post to fill
  In India's distant land.

On Jessy's heart the crushing stroke
  With cruel anguish fell ;
She felt, as parting words they spoke,
  'Twould be their last farewell.

No dreams of hope that sought to dwell
  On toils and dangers past,
Could break the sad foreboding spell
  O'er Jessy's spirit cast.

She felt that they should meet no more,
  Her life-star fled.   He went,
He safely reached far India's shore,
  And speedy tidings sent.

His letters lightened Jessy's woe,
  And soothed her lonely pain ;
But nought th' assurance could bestow
  That they should meet again.

Not e'en when after lapse of years
  His quick return drew near,
Could the bright prospect check her fears,
  Or her sad spirit cheer.

At length glad tidings came once more,
   And Jessy's hope revives ;
Tidings, that on his native shore
   Her darling William lives.

Rapid the hours successive move
   That bring her William near ;
Too slow—too tardy—for her love ;
   E'en now she hopes with fear.

At length her ear has faintly caught
   The wheels' approaching sounds,
And with a speed that falters not
   Along the path she bounds.

She reached the well-known river side,
   Nor here her footsteps stay,—
The yielding planks across the tide,
   Beneath her light tread lay.

One moment more, and they should meet,—
   She hears his well-known voice ;
And now with bliss her heart dares beat,
   Her spirit dares rejoice.

But, ah ! what means that fearful crash ?
   The railing falls beneath !
Her foot is slipping ! With a splash
   Poor Jessy sinks to death.

In vain, distracted, William shrieks,
    And help is promptly given;
No earthly sound death's slumber breaks—
    Sweet Jessy is in heaven.

RETURNING SPRING.

AY laughing over the mountains,
   I come,—the beautiful spring;
Unlocking the ice-bound fountains,
   Rich treasures of beauty I fling.

Winter may have been dreary,
   With its withered flower and tree;
And the spirit may have been weary
   That hath longed and pined for me.

But the book of Inspiration,
   With words of holy peace,
Hath whispered consolation,
   "The spring time shall not cease."

So I come to banish sadness
   Wherever my voice is heard.
And I come to waken gladness,
   With the music of brook and bird.

Let thy spirit drink the glory
    Beaming from earth and sky ;
As I tell the plea-ing story
    Of summer approaching nigh.

As I read the heaven-writ lesson,
    Inscribed on flower and tree ;
Let thine heart attentive listen,
    Its teachings are all for thee.

As now the glad sun is breaking
    Stern Winter's icy chain,
And the bright earth re-awaking
    To verdure and life again.

So shall the sun immortal
    Life-giving radiance pour,
And from the grave's dark portal
    The sleepers shall start once more.

And the winter of death shall vanish,
    As the re-awakening ray
All blight and decay shall banish
    With the summer of endless day.

RESIGNATION.

ORD! restrain my wayward will,
Speak my warring passions still;
Fill my breast with hallowed calm,
Soothe my griefs with holy balm.

Ever let my soul recline
On Thy promises divine;
And with resignation feel
Sweet submission to Thy will.

Though dark clouds are hovering round,
And though sorrows still abound,
And I see no glimmering ray
Speak the dawning of the day.

Can I not on Christ rely?
Is not He for ever nigh?
Nigh to cheer, direct, defend,
With me always to the end.

Yea, on Him my care I 'll cast,
Praise Him for His mercies past;
Trust Him still for what 's to come,
Till I safe arrive at home.

Then I 'll know and understand
How He led me by the hand,
Through thick clouds and darkness here,
To that bright and holy sphere.

There no darkness e'er shall be,—
Sorrow shall for ever flee ;
Saviour ! by Thy power sustain,
Till that glorious rest I gain.

THE MAIDEN'S SOLILOQUY.

F to hide away in the heart's deep core
    One unforgotten face,
  And to feel that there by resistless power
    Is daguerreotyped each trace ;
    If each changing look holds in secret spell
  The thoughts that would seek to rove,
If *this* be loving,—ay, far too well ;—
  Alas ! I fear I love.

If the sounds that break from those lips in words,
  May my heart's wild throbs command,
Awakening melody on its chords,
  Like a heavenly minstrel's hand ;
And if in vain to hush or to still
  Those trembling chords I have strove,—
If *this* is love's hand controlling the will,
  Alas ! I fear I love.

Come Reason! come Virtue! come honour's pride,
   Come Piety, brightest and best;
Come, steer aright over passion's tide
   The feelings that move my breast.
Tear away every idol that lurks within,
   Recall these affections that rove;
Guard me from error, and save me from sin,
   Teach me aright to love!

ON LOVE.

LOVE not too fondly.   Those thou lov'st may change,
    change,
    And hearts that now beat truly as thine
    own,
    Time's hand may rudely sever and estrange,
And thou be left to love and mourn alone.

And shouldst thou find a tried and faithful heart,
    On which thy treasured love may fondly rest,
Death's hand too soon the tender tie may part,
    And tear the cherished idol from thy breast.

And oh, beware !   Thy love may light on one
    Whose heart can ne'er responsive beat to thine ;
That passion pure, worthy high heaven alone,
    Be lavished on a thankless, earthly shrine.

And e'en the brightest, fairest flowers of earth,
    Live but to wither—bloom but to decay.
Though passing fair, yet of terrestrial birth,
    E'en while we gaze, their beauty fades away.

And must this passion pure, this gift of Heaven,
  Awake no thrill of transport in the breast?
Was this bright bower in vain to mortals given
  To tempt their feet to a forbidden rest?

No! One remains whom time can ne'er estrange,—
  One friend the hand of death can ne'er remove :
Then troubled heart, wearied of earthly change,
  Seek thy repose in God, for God is Love.

I MISS THEE.

OTHER! I miss thee when the morn
    Wakes all around to life and joy;
My heart is stricken and forlorn,
    I miss the love-light of thine eye.

I miss thee in the busy scene,
    Thy gentle look,—thine accents mild;
Thy smile that spoke of peace within,—
    Thy words that cheered and blessed thy child.

I miss thy gently guiding hand,
    That sought to train my wayward youth;
To lead me to the better land,
    Through paths of piety and truth.

I miss thee at the hour of prayer;
    My eye still seeks the accustomed place.
But, ah! in vain.   I miss thee there,
    And the calm faith that lit thy face.

I miss thee when with grief opprest
  My spirits sink. Thou mayst not now
Share in the sorrows of my breast,
  Or cool the fever of my brow.

Mother! I shall not miss thee when
  My spirit finds its home above.
I know that we shall meet again,
  In realms of purity and love.

AN ACROSTIC.

JOINED in spirit and in heart,
   O'er life's changing path we tread :
   Nor can time or distance part
   As we cleave to Christ our head.
   Still united, may we in His statutes tread.

Sheltered by the Rock of Ages
In this bleak and desert land,
Dreary though the tempest rages—
Doubts and dangers threatening stand,
Armed with panoply divine,
Lean upon thy Saviour's hand.
Leads to victory our Emmanuel.   Trust in His
      command.

As thou seek'st thine home in heaven,
Let thy faith and hope increase.
Love's pure joys to thee be given,
Earthly comforts,—heavenly peace :
New delights for ever springing ; endless
      happiness.

A WISH.

GIVE me a fireside where sweet peace and love
    Have fixed their abiding home ;
No splendours should tempt my ambition
    to rove,—
    No palace—my foot to roam.

Give me a table where Temperance presides,
    And deals out the pure repast ;
And I ask not the dainties that Wealth provides
    To pamper the craving taste.

Give me an honest, untarnished name,
    Which Virtue may smile to own ;
And I covet no " niche in the temple of fame,"
    No proud monumental stone.

Give me the sense of God's presence below,
    His pardoning love in my breast ;
His smile and His favour as heavenward I go,
    And I leave to His wisdom the rest.

TO CYNTHIA.

HAIL Cynthia! silver orb of night!
Hail with thy pure, reflected light!
Not dazzling as the sun's bright gleam,
But with unclouded, steady beam ;
Breathing sweet influence o'er my soul,
Its wilder passions to control.

Thy mild and gently-beaming ray
Shines on the loved ones far away ;
The glances I no more may meet,
Still drink, with mine, thine influence sweet.
Connecting link thou seem'st to be,
Smiling alike on them and me.

Oh ! teach us thus on life's dark path
To shed bright beams of love and faith ;
May holier links our hearts unite
Than the pale moon's inconstant light.
One Father's love, one Father's care,—
Alike we prove, alike we share.

THE HEAVENLY RACE.

UNNER in the heavenly race !
Gather courage—speed thy pace !
Nobly fling each weight away,
Not one moment loitering stay !

Pleasure's by-paths may invite,—
Glittering baubles meet thy sight,—
Sloth's inglorious couch appear ;—
Turn not ! pause not ! rest not here !

True ! the way is rough and long ;
True ! thine enemies are strong ;
And on direst end intent
Thy bright progress to prevent.

True ! the night of sorrow's cloud
May the darkening landscape shroud,
And the howling tempest spread
Wildly, fiercely round thy head.

True ! the narrow path to keep,
Thou must climb up many a steep.
Onward ! upward ! still aspire,
Start not back from flood or fire !

Rough and long the way may be,
Not too long or rough for thee
Whilst thy Saviour points the road,
By the path Himself has trod.

Enemies may gather round,
But with unseen chain all bound
He restrains them by His might,
He hath won for thee the fight.

Not one dart shall reach thy breast,
Of faith's glorious shield possest ;
Not one shock have power to move
Whilst protected by His love.

And in gloomiest, darkest hour,
Strength, and grace, and nerving power,
In rich measures shall be given,
As thine eye is fixed on heaven.

'Tis not always cloudy night ;
Many a beam of glorious light,
With celestial, heaven-lit ray
Kindles darkness into day.

E'en the conflict, fire, and flood,
All are needful for thy good;
And one hour of heaven's bright smile
Richly shall reward thy toil.

Lift thy tear-filled eye, and see
Spirit legions watching thee.
Lo! in shining throngs they stand,
Many a white-robed, seraph band.

Those that trod the same rough path.
Strengthened by the same strong faith,
Weak and helpless once as thou,—
Glory crowned, immortal now.

Hark! they urge thee to proceed
On thy path with tireless speed;
See! they beckon thee to wear
Yon bright crown that glitters there.

On then, runner! yet a while
Shun each tempter's deadly smile.
Onward! to the inviting skies;
Reach the goal! and seize the prize!

THE PARTING OF FRIENDS.

H ! the pain, the grief of parting
    With the friends we love so well !
Oh ! the heart-throbs wildly starting
    As we breathe the fond farewell.

When the joy-lit beam of gladness
    With their presence fades away ;
How the cold, dark cloud of sadness
    Dims the brightness of love's day !

Still more, when the strong resemblance
    To the loved ones in the tomb,
Breaks the floodgates of remembrance,
    And full tides of memories come—

Come with rushing, whelming power,
    Whispering of the distant past ;
Joys of many a blissful hour,
    Far too pure and bright to last.

But 'tis so !   Whilst here sojourning,
   Ever will the heart, alas !
In its hours of grief be yearning
   For the happiness that *was*.

But more lasting joys invite us,
   Where pure, kindred spirits dwell ;
Death itself shall re-unite us,—
   Heaven shall hear no sad farewell.

HOPE.

 SAW a mother weep for the loved one gone
    away,
    Now sleeping Death's long sleep, in the
    place of dark decay ;
    She showed me many a toy that the little
    hand had touched,
She spoke of many a joy that the early death had
    crushed.
She told the strong resemblance to her lovely, living
    child,
Save that to her fond remembrance, *that* was far more
    fair and mild.
But she said, as Hope's bright sunshine chased the sad-
    ness from her brow,
" I know that we shall meet again—my child is hap-
    pier now."

A parent, loved and honoured, lay down to droop and
    die ;
Her setting sun shone clearly in her life's calm evening
    sky.

She had long known blessed union with the spirit-world
    above,
And the hallowed sweet communion had so filled her
    heart with love
That it shone through every feature in virtue's beaming
    light—
And it purified her nature with heavenly graces bright.
And the tears that streamed from loving eyes her part-
    ing accents dried,
"We part a while to meet again beyond Death's solemn
    tide."

O Death! thine hand falls ruthlessly on all earth's
    tenderest ties;
The brightest, fairest, loveliest droops; the most be-
    loved one dies.
Alas! for loving, bleeding hearts! if this alone were
    home,
If no bright ray had pierced the darkness hanging o'er
    the tomb.
O Hope of Immortality! thy radiance pure and
    bright
Sheds o'er earth's fleeting, changing scenes, glad beams
    of heavenly light.
And thy blessed voice assures the heart, by parting
    anguish riven,
Of a land undimmed by Sorrow's clouds, of a meeting-
    place in heaven.

THE CITY "'BUS."

PICTURE for the artist, a study for the
sage,
  One of the liveliest sights of our busy,
    bustling age,
    Is the moving panorama the observing eye
      may meet
In the "'bus" that rolls its living freight along the
  city street.

Perchance you enter when the "coast is clear" save one
  or two,
Who courteously make room, and rather seem to welcome you ;
And now, to while away the time, you strive to scan
  the book
Of which each face presents a page—the varied human
  look.

A richly dressed prim lady sits erect in stately pride ;
And a mother, with her darling boy, glad smiling, by
  her side ;

Oh! might the future ever find that smile as pure and
    free !
Oh! might that happy heart untouched by guilt and
    sorrow be !

Dong! sounds the bell, and up comes one, with slow
    and steady pace,
Deliberate firmness stamped on every feature of his face;
The dignity of motion in the eye, the foot, the hand,
Bespeaks a mind unused to serve, accustomed to com-
    mand.

Next comes a bright-eyed damsel, gentle, modest, young,
    and fair ;
Now a youth, affecting manhood, struts with conse-
    quential air ;
And now a merry party dash in briskly one and all,
Perchance intent on " shopping," or on friendly, social
    call.

With pleasant chat they waken silence into cheery sound,
And a catching air of mirthfulness seems spreading all
    around ;
And gracefully or grumblingly the passengers make
    room,
And seats " *impossible*" are found as fresh arrivals come.

Now enters one whose sable garb proclaims a loved
    one dead,
Wearing the mark of widowhood upon her silv'ry head;

She fain would hide the lonely thoughts that o'er her
    features play,
But now and then a trickling tear *will* find its down-
    ward way.

Oh! who can guess the hopes, the fears, the transports,
    or the cares,
That (all unconscious of its load) the rattling "'bus"
    now bears?
Each life a hist'ry only known to Him who reads the
    heart—
Each heart a deep mysterious scroll unread by human
    art;

Each soul the centre of a power, whose radii, unconfined,
Extend immeasurably round, leaving our thoughts be-
    hind;
Each working out some good or ill, whose influence
    shall extend
Beyond the reach of mortal ken, where Time itself shall
    end.

" Fares, please!"—The reverie is broken! Pockets,
    purses, hands,
Are quickly all astir, to satisfy the guard's demands;
We wheel around, and then stand still, then separate,
    and thus
We end our ride and musings in the busy city "'bus."

AUTUMN MUSINGS.

 WAS an early autumn morning,
   And I wandered forth a while—
Forth to catch the golden glory
   Of the summer's parting smile.

Unaccustomed gloom had shrouded
   Many a long and dreary day;
And the mourning flowers had withered,
   Pining for the sun's bright ray.

And the darkness, clouds, and showers,
   Many a heart had filled with dread,
For the blighted hopes of harvest
   That in many a field lay spread.

But the sunshine once more streaming
   Seemed a message from above,
That the Father still remembered
   His dependent ones in love.

All looked bright as lovely spring-time
  Save the leaves of russet brown ;
Which the freshening, sportive breezes
  Shook in rustling showers down.

But unlike the spring's sweet influence,
  Something of a pensive cast,
Feelings tinged with melancholy
  O'er my musing spirit passed.

For the trees so lately blooming
  In their varied summer hues,
For the winter were disrobing ;
  And I grieved their charms to lose.

Laying by their withering garments,
  In the wardrobe of the earth,
Till resuscitating nature
  Gives them new and vernal birth.

Thus succeeding budding spring-time,
  And the summer's glorious bloom,
Ever will the autumn's fading
  And the winter's darkness come.

But, methinks, love's links grow stronger
  As the summer charms expire,
And methinks our hearts draw closer
  As we pile the winter's fire.

Every season hath its pleasures,
  Every season hath its gloom ;
Bliss unmixed, perennial, lasting,
  Dwells alone beyond the tomb.

WORK AND WAIT.

NOT all at once doth the broad flowing river
    Leap in its mightiness forth to the day,
Sweeping along, in proud majesty ever,
    On to the ocean away and away.
    Many a cloudlet kissed up by the sunbeam
Must float and commingle, condense and descend ;
Many a streamlet must sparkle with bright gleam,
  And towards one deep channel each silvery course
    bend—
Small in its source as the rills that surround it,
  In wild mountain solitudes springing to light ;
Yet, fed and enriched by the waters around it,
  It becometh a wonder of vastness and might.

Not all at once to their marvellous greatness
  Do the tall forest trees grandly arise ;
Not by some process of magical fleetness
  Raise they their towering heads towards the skies.
Many an acorn hath fallen and mouldered,
  Trodden—forgotten—apparently dead ;

But within it the germ of a new life hath smouldered,
  Till it heaved its clay tomb, and uprose from its bed.
And many a young, tender shoot hath been nourished
  By the dews and the showers which kind Nature
      hath given;
And through ages of sunshine and storm wind hath
      flourished,
  And now waves its time-honoured branches towards
      heaven.

Not all at once have earth's mightiest nations
  Raised their proud trophies of freedom and power;
Strongly and deeply were laid the foundations
  In blood and in conflict in terror's dark hour.
'Midst tyranny's rule and hot-headed rebellions,
  The angel of progress hath winged her glad flight;
And patriots have bled for the rights of the millions,
  And their blood proved the seed for a harvest of light;
And knowledge and virtue together descended,
  Enlightening, ennobling, and blessing the land;
And commerce and art, and refinement were blended,
  To crown it with dignity, might, and command.

Oh! ye who are earnestly, longingly yearning
  For the bright blessings the future conceals,
Ever be hopefully, trustfully learning
  Lessons from all that the bygone reveals.
Not all at once shall the wrongs which oppress us
  Lose their keen sting, or be robbed of their power;
Not all at once shall the woes which distress us
  Yield to the brightness of Joy's sunlit hour.

Stream after stream its bright tribute is bringing ;
  Rolls the river of knowledge its deepening tide ;
Seed after seed Truth is ceaselessly flinging,
  And trees of immortal fruit bloom by its side.

Thousands of thirsty souls, eagerly thronging,
  Come to the bright sparkling water to drink ;
Thousands of famished ones, hungrily longing,
  Pluck the blest life-giving fruits on its brink.
Tyranny, error, and darkness are holding
  Partially, feebly, their fast-ending sway,
Soon shall the future, in glorious unfolding,
  Chase all their mists and their fetters away.
Hastening that time, let us all toil unceasing ;
  And though not in our day be the bright reward given,
Others unborn shall awake to its blessings,
  When we, still more blest, rest for ever in heaven.

LINES ON THE DEATH OF A HOME MISSIONARY.

A LIGHT hath beamed around us with more
    than earthly ray ;
    It caught its fadeless brilliance from the
    fount of endless day ;
    It gleamed amidst the darkness of sin and
sorrow's gloom,
Where the desolate and weary pined in their cheerless
    home ;
It hath kindled anew Hope's brightness in the tear-
    dimmed, grief-worn eye ;
It hath shone round the bed of anguish, where the suf-
    ferer lay down to die ;
It hath guided many a footstep to the haven of endless
    rest ;—
'Twas the light of heaven enkindled on the shrine of a
    loving breast.
Mourn ! ye that have felt its influence ; it hath passed
    from earth away ;
It hath gone as a star to glitter in the blaze of eternal
    day.

A stream hath glided by us with gentle, noiseless roll,
And hath borne salvation's waters to many a thirsting
    soul;
Where in sin's burning desert the serpent-bitten lay,
They have tasted the healing nectar, and the curse hath
    fled away;
And where blight and desolation long held their dreary
    reign,
Those bright reviving waters have rewakened life again.
That stream was the overflowing of the love-spring in
    the heart,
That sought to dying mortals undying hopes to impart.
Mourn! ye whose throbbing bosoms have been healed
    by its tide of love,
It hath entered eternity's ocean in that brighter world
    above.

Yes! mourn for the light and the love that away from
    earth have passed;
But the holy, mighty influence of a good man's life shall
    last;
Far richer than the spices that emba'med old Egypt's
    kings,
Is the fragrant, heartfelt tribute that affection fondly
    brings;
And costlier than the honours on Fame's favourites
    proudly shed,
Are the tear drops that shall water the good man's
    grassy bed;
And the memory of his virtues, in many a bosom sown,
Shall bring forth fruit to ripen round the eternal throne.

CHRISTMAS-TIDE.

THERE are seasons that call a glad nation out,
  To the joy of a festival time,
When the merry bells answer the people's
        shout,
    With their musical clang and chime ;
And the banners are floating bright and gay
  On the melody-laden air,
On the birth, or the bridal, or crowning day
  Of the throne's true, rightful heir ;
Or when victory's hand hath the laurels bound
  On the hero's triumphant brow,
How the multitudes blazon his fame around !
  And to Fortune's favourite bow !
But a world-wide joy is Christmas-tide,
  And a world its welcome sings ;
It hails not the glory of earthly pride,
  But the birth of the King of kings.

There are joys that awaken childhood's voice
  To the mirth of a jubilant hour ;

But they bid not the old man's heart rejoice,
  Over him they have lost their power ;
And perchance on the ear of the busy man
  They grate with discordant sound,
His joy is to make and to count his gains,
  When credit and wealth abound.
And even the aged heart may thrill
  When some old familiar tone,
Of one of youth's comrades, remaining still,
  Shall talk of the days long flown.
But alike to old, to busy, to young,
  Old Christmas new joy can impart ;
And the heaven-taught anthem, the angels' song,
  Finds echoes in every heart.

It flingeth around—free, unconfined,
  A general festive call ;
It serves as a golden link to bind
  The hearts and the hopes of all.
The songs of heaven resound from earth,
  For the angels of Bethlehem's plain
Still pour their unceasing praises forth
  To the Saviour's honoured name.
Rich, poor, old, young, black and white, catch the
      strain ;
  Heaven and earth spread the joy far and wide ;
For glory to God and good-will unto man,
  Is the theme of the Christmas-tide.

THE PEN AND THE PRESS.

TRONG is the might of the warrior's hand,
    As he graspeth his trusty sword,
And joineth the hosts that embattled stand
    Where life's current is lavishly poured ;
And strong are the floating bulwarks that
        ride
On the breast of the dancing wave,
Where in deadly conflict the brave decide
    For victory—or the grave !
But stronger than army and fleet combined
    Is the power of liberty,
In the land where no hand may dare fetter the mind,
    Where the pen and the press are free.

Clothed with a solemn and dreadful awe
    Are the terrors stern Justice wears,
Enforcing the doom of a broken law
    With the power that she grandly bears.
But the monarch that ruleth by force alone,
    And maketh his strength his trust,

But sits on a feeble and tottering throne,
  Which a storm may lay in the dust.
Progress, and safety, and glory, and light,
  Alone in that land can be
Where the throne is upheld by the people's might,
  And the pen and the press are free.

Oh ! the busy pen ! how it traceth out
  The flights of the busier mind,
Which, roaming through regions of lofty thought,
  Leaves a shining trace behind.
And the teeming press,—how it flings around
  The rainbow-wreaths of truth,
The sparkling genius, or lore profound,
  Of wise age or of ardent youth !
God grant that our land may still remain
  The glory of earth and sea ;
And from tyranny's chain, and from error's stain,
  May our pen and our press be free !

A FAREWELL TO THE OLD YEAR.

DING dong!—Ding dong! Toll deep, and
      loud, and long ;
    For another old year is dying ;
    His last moments are swiftly flying ;
    On the night winds his farewells are
      sighing,
And the mournful bells are replying,
Farewell ! Ding ! dong ! dong !

Ah ! Gone ! gone ! gone ! is many a hope he brought :
    And many a heart is turning,
    With a passionate longing, yearning,
    To the joys fled past returning,
    And in life's stern school is learning
Lessons by changes taught.

Ding ! dong ! ding ! dong ! Toll for the dreary homes
    Where the death-angel's wing hath been lighting,
    And with pestilence darkly blighting,

With terror-winged dart affrighting,
Or with sudden dread-stroke smiting
The loved to the greedy tomb.

The worn old year is closing the solemn pages—
Life's mystic records showing,
For our future fuller knowing.
And now he is rapidly going,
And with Time's ceaseless current flowing
To the ocean of by-gone ages.

The old year dies, and makes way for another to come,
His mission and work is ended—
With the tales of the past he hath blended ;
But we trust by our God defended,
By His Guardian Love attended,
That our last shall bear us safe home.

REQUIEM.

NOTHER laid to sleep,
    That slumber long and deep,
    In the silence Death doth keep,
Beyond the power of earthly breaking :
    Thunders may peal around,
  Earthquakes may shake the ground,
  Locked in that sleep profound,
Those eyes shall know no earthly waking.

    Another life web span,—
    Another life task done,—
    Another life race run,—
Another crossed the changeful ocean ;
    Another bark at rest
    In the harbour's tranquil breast,
    Where all is calm and blest,
After the tossing waves' commotion.

X

Thus one by one we go
Through earthly weal or woe,
Borne on by Time's swift flow,
Whose onward rolling stayeth never ;
Thus one by one we explore
That mystic far-off shore,
Where, all our wanderings o'er,
Our souls shall find the vast " for ever."

Another solemn stone
In the quiet churchyard lone
Shall speak a loved one gone,
Reminding us that we are mortal ;
But whilst affection grieves,
Our faith-taught hope believes
He is not dead, but lives ;—
He passed through Death to gain Life's portal.

ST VALENTINE.

WHATE'ER St Valentine could be—
 Or rich, or poor; or grave, or gay;
Or how inclined for love was he,
 I think there are but few can say.

Whate'er he was,—now, at his shrine
 Is kindled many a latent flame;
And many a tender love-fraught line
 Is graced with his time-honoured name.

And though we mourn that British skill
 Should e'er unseemly prints devise
The place of chaste designs to fill,
 And catch youth's giddy, heedless eyes;

Yet not alone for this sole crime,
 From yearly records would we blot
All traces of this festive time,
 By love and friendship unforgot.

For surely wishes fond and kind
 For others' good or others' peace,
Chains that each heart may closer bind,
 Can ne'er be wrong, or out of place.

And whilst to taste, design, and skill,
 Is offered a lucrative sphere ;
For this, we gladly welcome still
 St Valentine from year to year.

And then,—what sums in figures round
 It yields the country's coffers !   May
More galling taxes ne'er be found
 Than those Love's votaries freely pay

And may our youth with motives pure,
 Nor word, nor sentiment e'er send,
But such as may truth's light endure.
 And beautify the name of friend

THE FIRSTBORN.

FOND mother! blooming still in youth's first
        charms,
  And painting visions bright
  For the fair sleeper cradled in thine arms,
    In robes of flowing white.

Of all the little helpless sons of earth,
  Not one so sweet and fair—
Not one to thee can match *his* priceless worth—
  Thy firstborn sleeping there.

Yes! 'tis the first whose little plaintive cry
  Hath stirred thine heart's deep chords,
To tenderness unknown in days gone by,
  To love too great for words.

The first frail tendril, twining firm and fast
  Around the parent stem;
The brightest joy-beam o'er thy life yet cast—
  Thy richest earthly gem.

Aye tend it watchfully ; its worth untold,
  Demands thine utmost care ;
Before its value heaps of glittering gold
  Lighter than feathers are.

Look not upon it merely as a toy,
  The plaything of an hour ;
Hidden within the bosom of thy boy
  Lie seeds of mighty power.

This little tiny shoot Time's hand may rear
  Into a stalwart tree,
Life-giving foliage and fruits to bear,
  Or poisonous food to be.

This little stream, so tiny in its source,
  May bless the thirsty ground ;
Or, darkly wandering from its destined course,
  Spread desolation round.

The soul that animates that lovely clay—
  That spark of heavenly light—
Must live unquenched through everlasting day,
  Or never-ending night.

Mother ! 'tis thine to teach thine infant son
  A country's hope to be ;
Mother ! 'tis thine to train a deathless one
  For immortality.

Oh ! curb his growing will from day to day,
   And seek, in earliest youth,
Upon his wakening thoughts to pour the ray
   Of pure, celestial truth.

With careful hand pluck up the springing weeds
   Of selfishness and pride ;
Teach him that, spite of differing grades and creeds,
   Mankind are all allied.

Although thy firstborn and thy darling son,
   Let him not fondly deem
Himself the chief and all-important one,
   And earth made but for him.

Teach him, by noble sacrifice of self,
   To seek to bless his kind—
To rise above the sordid love of pelf,
   Virtue's reward to find.

Tell him that life is a vast battle-field
   Betwixt the wrong and right ;
Teach him Truth's arms in Freedom's cause to wield,
   And valiantly to fight.

Mother ! no idle and ignoble task
   Is with this infant given ;
Go ! in thy weakness, kneel, and humbly ask
   Guidance and help from Heaven.

ANNIVERSARY HYMN.

HARK ! how Nature's thousand voices
    One harmonious concert raise ;
See ! the smiling earth rejoices
    To proclaim Jehovah's praise.
    Songs are rising all around us,
From the meadow, grove and brook ;
All the beauties that surround us,
    Are the notes in Nature's book.
Join we then Creation's chorus,
    Each with vocal heart and tongue ;
Whilst beneath us, round us, o'er us,
    Swells the universal song.

Hark ! diviner strains outpouring,
    Rise earth's loudest notes above ;
Ransomed sinners are adoring
    Infinite ! unbounded Love !
Mightier truths than Nature teacheth,
    In the gospel spring to light ;
And the love-tuned spirit reacheth
    To a loftier, holier flight.

Join we then redemption's chorus,
    Raise we here our loudest strain ;
Swell the anthem floating o'er us,
    Worthy is the Lamb once slain !

Hark ! the glorified are singing,
    Yonder bright and blood-washed throng ;
And through heaven's arches ringing,
    Peals the loud triumphant song.
Earthly discords cannot enter,
    Not one jarring string find place ;
Love the key-note, Christ the centre,
    And the theme, redeeming grace.
Join we then the angelic chorus,
    Learn the new eternal song ;
Soon with loved ones gone before us
    We shall swell that white-robed throng.

WOMAN.

OMAN ! what is she ? or what should she be ?
Fit theme for sage, but daring one for me.
Problem of ages, still in interest new,—
Discussed by many, understood by few ;
How shall my weak, unskilful fingers trace
The glowing beauties, or the winning grace ?
Varied in each ?   As in a gay parterre,
Enriched with summer's glories brightly fair,
The queenly rose, adorned in regal pride,
Smiles on the fragrant lily at her side ;
The stately tulip lifts her gaudy head,
And rivals in her bloom the poppy red ;
The sunflower turns to heaven her constant gaze,
Attracted ever by the solar rays ;
Whilst fairer, though more lowly, from their bed
The modest violets sweetest perfume shed ;
Thus each bright flower discloses beauties new,
But all unite to charm the ravished view.
So, varied as the countless forms she wears
To countless eyes, yet woman still appears

The flower that sheds its sweetness over life,
The charming maiden, or the tender wife ;
Or mother to whose watchful care 'tis given •
To tend the bud that may expand in heaven.
Whether the rose's bloom or lily's grace
With purity and beauty deck her face—
Or, less attractive to the eye than mind,
The violet's sweetness in her life we find—
Still woman wields a spirit-softening power,
The poetry of life, the garden's flower ;
Where'er *she* dwells, a hallowed spot is found,
And fragrant influences hover round.

This as the rule ; but still we own there are
Exceptions sad—would that they were more rare !
When error-chained in judgment and in thought,
Her mission and her duties all forgot,
She sacrifices hopes and joys divine
On Fashion's altar and on Folly's shrine.
When self-indulgence palsies heart and brain,
And empty pleasures leave the sting of pain ;
When, tempted by the specious arts of vice,
She seeks in turn the unwary to entice,
And sinks, if no kind hand be stretched to save,
A wreck of loveliness, 'neath ruin's wave.

If, then, her power for good or ill so great,—
If such the dangers on her steps that wait,-
Is it not needful that the means be known
How *that* to understand, and *these* to shun ?
Since, though at first created good and pure,

Yet not from guile infallibly secure;
Our general mother, trusting Reason's ray,
Instead of Truth's bright guidings, missed her way,
And left a mournful legacy below,
Which history and experience jointly show
Her daughters share alike—proneness to err,
And wander in forbidden paths like her.

What then should woman be?—how trained, how led,
Rightly her part to play, her path to tread?
What bright examples may her soul inspire,
And fill her breast with emulous desire?
Shall martial glory spread its specious charms,
And lure her to the din and clash of arms?
Precedents we may find in history's page,
In many a country, and in many an age,
When female patriotism has sought the field,
And woman's courage forced the foe to yield.
Thus Israel's Deborah, at the army's head,
The doubting Barak on to victory led;
Thus Italy's fair Countess, pure, refined,
Aldrude, of noble form, and nobler mind,
The calls of generosity obeyed,
And lent distressed Ancona timely aid;
Thus Boadicea, on her island throne,
Stung by her people's wrongs and by her own,
Led her brave Britons forth to meet the foe—
Ill-fated queen, destined to grief and woe!
Her force before superior numbers failed,
The more disciplined Roman ranks prevailed.
She died; but blazoned on the scroll of fame,

Inscribed amongst the brave we find her name.
And France, too, when war's thunders shook her
    throne,
And foreign hands were grasping at her crown,
Can boast her Orleans Maid, who, heaven-inspired,
The fainting spirits of her army fired ;
Freedom and victory to her land she gave,
But found a strange return,—a stake and grave.
Philippa, too, and Margaret, stand enrolled
In England's annals for achievements bold.
Yet though Philippa quelled the Scottish strife,
We more admire her as the pleading wife,
When to her tears and prayers stern Edward gave
Life to the doomed, and pardon to the brave.
These challenge admiration, in so far
As circumstances called them forth to war;
But that fair woman's hand should wield the sword
Is equally by head and heart abhorred.
Before *her* presence broils and feuds should cease ;
Her name should be the sign and guard of peace.
But equal courage should her mind engage,
To battle with the follies of the age ;
To stand unmoved by giant Custom's might,
And, having chosen, to defend the right,
A heroine in virtue's cause to shine,
Enduring laurels round her brow shall twine.

Say, then, with high resolve and purpose great,
Shall woman mingle in the affairs of state ?
Ought she, by right and fitness, in its care
To rival man, and equal powers to share ?

Here, too, as precedents, bright names we find,
Whose steps have left a shining track behind.
Great Catherine lived, a mother to her land,
And governed Russia with a skilful hand.
Elizabeth, of glorious memory,
(Though not from human imperfections free,)
With firm, strong hand, and cool, discerning head,
To Truth's bright light a darkened nation led.
Omitting many a fair unmentioned name,
Last, but not least, a foremost place we claim
For HER whose rule extends o'er land and flood,
Wide, far, and near,—VICTORIA THE GOOD.
But scarce, like female warriors of our scene;
Not generally, but few and far between,
Are women raised to posts of eminence,
The laws to frame or justice to dispense.
The few who *are* show what the many *can ;*
Not much inferior they in mind to man.
But gentler, more unfit to toil or roam,
Fair woman reigns the queen of sacred home ;
It wisdom needs, and prudence quite as great,
To govern rightly here as in a state.
We think true-hearted woman will find here
This her legitimate and proper sphere.
A mighty power is hers, to sway the mind
By reason and persuasion aptly joined,
Though properly denied the right to sit
In public in the legislator's seat.
If nobleness and virtue fill *her* soul,
Here she may exercise a sage control,
And by love's force insensibly command

Decisions in the hearts that rule the land.
This *her* prerogative, and happy she
Who knows to guide, and yet submissive be.

Nor let our heroine vainly seek to throw
O'er nature's charms the veil of tinsel show ;
Love of display most generally we find
To evidence deficiency of mind.
If beauty's winning bloom adorn her face,
She needs to seek no artificial grace.
And if it lack the spell of beauty's power,
Profuse adornments show the want still more.
Good sense and modesty alike declare
To the well-tutored taste what garb to wear ;
So suited to complexion, age, and state,
As no undue attention to create.
'Tis far beneath her native dignity,
A slave to Fashion's fickle whims to be.

Nor let her seek in Pleasure's giddy round
The happiness alone in virtue found.
All that creates or feeds a wish to roam,
Is traitorous to the peace of holy home ;
'Tis dangerous to indulge the roving thought
That draws the affections from that central spot.
In life's wild ocean, HOME should be the ark—
Were its light quenched, all else indeed were
    dark ;
Then, save when health or duty calls abroad,
Here be her treasures and her cares bestowed.

As to acquirements—all, we think, whose aim
Is high and virtuous, justly she may claim.
Where talent, skill, or genius is bestowed,
What path of knowledge is forbidden road ?
So far as opportunity and time
Allow, let her with fearless footsteps climb
The hill of science, where a clearer sky
Shall light new scenes to charm the enraptured eye.
The more she lives within the world of mind,
The more she leaves earth's sensual chains behind,
The ignorant, uncultured heart obeys
Its circumstances, and long, weary days
Drags out in listlessness, dependent made
On casual novelties, and outward aid.
Dress—gossip—trifles—each in turn is tried,
And yet the inward want, unsatisfied,
Craves for some brighter toy, some newer scene,
To fill the void that still remains within.
But knowledge, rightly lodged within the breast,
Gives to the hungry soul a constant feast.
Far from unfitting for life's needful cares,
It sweetens toil, and lonely moments cheers,
And brings the wisdom of the past to bear
To soothe and smooth the path of rugged care.

Not only should she wealth of wisdom gain,
But guard the outlet of the busy brain.
Well it behoves with barriers safe and strong,
To fence and check the ever-ready tongue,
Which, unrestrained, to such wild lengths might go,
As in one hour to work a life-time's woe.

The fewest words bespeak the greatest sense,
The ripest thoughts, in fewest words condense.
As far from slander as from vile deceit,
Let Truth and Wisdom in her accents meet;
Transparent, may she *feel* all they convey,
And yet, not *all she thinks*, impulsive say.
Let well-weighed motives, words as actions move,-
The law of kindness, and the claims of love.

Chiefly let piety adorn her brow,
With purity that dwells not else below.
Distrustful of herself, a suppliant meek,
Let her Divine direction ever seek ;
Had thus fair Eve, in that sad, fatal hour,
Though strong in innocence and native power,.
Leaned for support on the Almighty arm,
The serpent's dart had lost its power to harm.
Trusting her heart, she fell beneath his hand,
Trusting their God, her weaker daughters stand.

Hail, pure religion ! by the Bible taught,
With elevating influences fraught !
Where thy bright beams illume the happy land,
There woman takes her highest, noblest stand.
Dark, senseless creeds her dignity destroy,
Sink her to slave, or treat her as a toy,
But thou hast loosed the chains that error bound—
She stands man's equal, on Faith's common ground.
Thy Founder and thy Lord, whilst here on earth,
Failed not to recognise her modest worth.

Y

The widow shrinking from the public eye
To give her mites, He passed not heedless by ;
He saw the love-spring of the generous deed,
And bright memorial of the act decreed.
And the forgiven one, whose grateful love
Sought by what means its strength and depth to
    prove,
That washed his feet with tears, then meekly dried
Those feet with her rich locks, so late her pride ;
Then costly ointment poured with eager haste,
Whilst hard, cold, avarice murmured at the
    waste ;
Its murmuring fell unheeded on her ear,
As His kind accents banished all her fear,
And spoke her deed accepted and approved,—
Much He forgave, and therefore much she loved.
And when in nature's last dread agony
He hung aloft on the accursed tree,
There faithful woman stood, powerless to aid,
And the dread scene with crushing grief surveyed.
He turned in death His languid, glazing eye,
And saw His much-loved mother standing by ;
And ere the waning sands of life had run,
Gave her a home,—a guardian,—and a son.
And when triumphantly He rose again,
O'er death's dread realm a conqueror to reign,
To woman first His risen form appeared,
And woman first His well-known accents cheered.

And Britain, hail ! Thou fairest land on earth !
Where Freedom's sons receive their happy birth !

Within thy social circles woman shines,
Their manners soften, and their tone refines.
Not to some Turkish hiding-place removed,
Nor worshipped as a goddess, but beloved;
Into society's great heart received,
Her honour trusted, and her truth believed,
And, as a rule, that truth and honour stand
The glory and the beauty of our land;
Which owes its greatness, not to strength alone,
Nor to the warriors that defend its throne,
But to the gentler elements that blend
With the great whole, cementing power to lend.
On every side *her* skill and industry
In thousand apt appliances we see;
Her cultured taste hath countless charms designed,
Firmer to home the admiring heart to bind;
Where pain and weary suffering press the bed,
She tends the couch and soothes the aching head;
When streaming eyes are weeping tears of grief,
Her gentle sympathy gives sweet relief;
When philanthropic schemes are brought to light,
Her heart and hands embrace them with delight;
Her quick-contriving, cheerful aid is brought,
To clothe in generous deeds the generous thought;
Even the outcast poor, whose tattered dress
Serves but to show, not hide, their wretchedness,
Sunk low, but not beyond *her* power to reach,
To these she seeks a Saviour's love to teach;
And sin-seared hearts, once cold and hard as
    stone,
  Her tears have softened, and her prayers have won.

Then hail, blest England ! where thy daughters stand
The guardian angels of their happy land.
The queen that wears thy crown, and fills thy throne,
Stands not in virtue, though in rank, alone.
Her bright example thousands hath inspired,
And with admiring emulation fired,
And countless homes of Britons brave and free,
Reflect the throne's unsullied purity.

Though much of earnest toiling still remains,
Ere all are freed from Guilt and Error's chains,
Though many a gloomy spot of heathen night
Awaits the beams of Truth's awakening light ;
Though many a giant evil lifts its head,
And stalks abroad with heaven-defying tread ;
Yet a pure leaven works its silent way—
We hail the dawning of a brighter day.
Untiring zeal, and perseverance strong,
Have nerved great hearts to battle with the wrong ;
And in the foremost ranks to bless her race,
Woman hath claimed, and still must hold her place—
Must seek to pour celestial light abroad,
True to herself, her country, and her God.

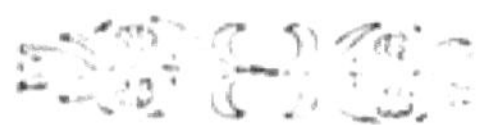

THE DREAM OF GOLD.

EARIED in foot, and hand, and heart, and
      brain,
With labour, and with discontented pain,
A murmurer sat, and heaped in scanty pile
The well-earned recompense of honest toil.
Late had those earnings been the pride of life,
As, fitly portioned by a frugal wife,
His home with untold comfort they had stored,
And welcomed hunger to the well-spread board.
But now a thirst for wealth has seized his heart,
And pierced his happiness with poisonous dart ;
He spurned mild Patience with her sage control,
And longed to reach at once the dazzling goal.
His hearth, so late the scene of dear delight,
To his dimmed eye lost its accustomed light ;
Compared with lordly mansions of the great,
He scorned his humbler home and lowlier state.
Long thus he sat indulging gloomy thought,
And vain repinings at his destined lot ;

Till his sad spirit felt a sudden change,
Impelled through newly-opening scenes to range.
He heard a voice inviting him to roam,
And, following, left behind his peaceful home.
" Thy wish is granted," said his unknown guide ;
" The workings of thy heart I 've long descried.
Come ! join the countless votaries at my shrine,
And all thy soul desires shall soon be thine !"
Thus spoke the strange unknown, and led the way
To where old Ocean's bosom heaving lay ;
He hailed a ship, with snowy wings outspread,
And to its deck the wondering wanderer led.
" Now, go !" cried he, " and seek the land of gold,
And be thy toil repaid by wealth untold !
We part a while, but thou the boon shalt gain,
And in the future we shall meet again."
Now wafted by a favouring wind's light wing,
The vessel glided like a living thing—
Favoured alike by wave, and breeze, and sky—
But yet too slow for his too eager eye ;
To him the waves' deep whisperings ever rolled
The echo of his thoughts,—the cry for gold.
Each night brought dreams of shining stores at
        hand ;
Each morn awoke him to a search for land.
At length, adorned with charms and beauties new,
The lovely landscape opened to his view.
And soon with feverish haste he sought and found
The spot where glittering dust enriched the ground ;
And late and early at the pleasing toil
He rifled earth and seized the precious spoil.

Success marked every effort ; and his store
So grew, that Avarice could not covet more.
Nuggets o'erlooked by many an anxious eye
Increased his gains and fed his new-found joy.
So fared he.   Rich in gold, and hope, and health,
Till princes might have coveted his wealth.
And now the question stirred his heart at length,
" Wherefore here longer squander life and strength ? "
Straightway the scene of toil and gain he leaves,
To seize and mould the shapes that Fancy weaves ;
Again a favouring bark unfurls the sail,—
Again she flies before a favouring gale.
Not less impatient he to reach his home,
Than once in haste to distant shores to roam.
He reached it ; and his wondrous story told,
And vouched its truth by shining heaps of gold.
And now a form his long-nursed visions found,
A princely palace crowned a rising ground.
Here Nature's charms with lavish Art combined
To chain the sense and captivate the mind ;
Taste, luxury, grandeur, ease, adorned each room,
Rich light streamed down through rainbow-coloured
        dome ;
Fruits of all lands, and fair exotic flowers,
Here drew the eye,—and there sweet shady bowers,
And where wide undulating acres lie,
Lawns, meadows, woods, lakes, fountains charmed
        the eye ;
Truly might gratified ambition ween
That earth a second paradise had seen.
And now contriving, planning, toiling o'er,

Safely invested his redundant store ;
Obsequious servants waiting on his nod,
And wealth and rank to greet his walks abroad,
He hoped, this summit reached, all cares should
    cease,
And life become one rosy bower of peace.
Brief seemed the time for rest and ease allowed,
When at his door, imperiously loud,
His bell announced a visitor, who came
Unbidden, and unknown his rank or name ;
He with familiar step the house explored,
And sought the presence of its wondering lord.
" I come," said he, " led hither by the friend
Who deigned to thee such wondrous power to lend,
MAMMON *his* name, and *mine* is pale DISEASE,
Invoked and wooed by luxuries such as these."
" Ah ! get thee gone !" the startled victim cried ;
" I charge thee, quit my door, with thy false guide ;
Or stay thine hand,—the cruel blow forbear !
If gold will bribe thee, thou shalt freely share
My wealth."   " No !" cried Disease, with stern, cold
    eye,
" Me never gold may bribe, or riches buy,—
Keep them to ease the sting of mortal pain ;
Take THAT ! and THAT !" and blows fell thick as rain.
His strength dried up, and inward fever burned ;
And from his door the spectre pale returned,
But left behind a deadly, poisoned dart,
That rankled in the sick and aching heart.
And now the long-desired and safe-reached goal
Seemed wormwood to his weary, fainting soul.

No rest nor ease, for body or for mind,
Could medicine give, or nice invention find.
Life, late a triumph, now a burden grown,
Wrings from his labouring breast full many a groan.
Thus day by day, and week by week rolls on,
His life-lamp quivering, and hope's prospects flown.
At length another warning at the door
Brings an unwelcome visitor once more ;
MAMMON now entered, and with him allied,
Though yet unseen, DEATH glided by his side.
Unled, he wound his way, and found the bed,
Whose downy pillows failed to ease the head.
Up starts the sufferer, with astonished gaze,
To see the treacherous guide of former days :
" We meet again !" cried he, " each boon bestowed,—
All that thou sought'st is thine ; this rich abode,
With all the appliances of splendid ease,
And every prospect that the eye can please.
I taught thee how to gain thy princely store,
Till e'en thy craving spirit asked no more ;
And now I wait thy thanks."   " What ! thanks to
          thee ?
Begone ! and henceforth cease to trouble me !
Or back restore those peaceful hours of old,
And give me ease beyond the power of gold.
Hadst thou not lured me from my happy home,
In a wild, maddening search for wealth to roam,
Perchance more humble, but more truly blest,
I ne'er had known the worm that gnaws my breast.
Begone ! or if it lie within thy power,
Give me my cot, my health, my peace once more !"

" Ungrateful wretch !" cried MAMMON, " thus to greet
My promised visit ; and, where thanks are meet,
To pour reproaches, undeservèd all !
I only came in answer to thy call.
Long hadst thou sought me,—long hadst inly pined
The shortest road to affluence to find.
This now possessing, thou upbraid'st thy guide,
Still with thine envied lot dissatisfied ;
But since I fail in all my gifts to please,
I bring thee one whose power may give thee ease,
And lay thine head, racked with distempered woes,
In slumbers sounder than blest childhood knows."
He spoke, and straightway starting into view,
The monster DEATH forth from his quiver drew
A poisoned arrow ;—and loud piercing cries
From the doomed helpless victim wildly rise.
He strives to fly the dread and fatal dart,—
He prays some power protection to impart ;
But all in vain for help he looks around,
Or strives to fly ; for as with fetters bound
The coil of unconfessed, unshriven sin
In serpent form entwines and shuts him in,
And strikes its deadly fangs into his heart,
Defencelessly exposed to DEATH's dread dart.
Cold, bead-like drops of sweat unheeded roll,
And racking anguish seizes on his soul,
Till from the doom impending o'er his head
He wildly starts ;—and lo ! the vision fled !
Amazed, he gazes round with mute surprize,
No glittering palace met his wondering eyes,
No liveried servants on his pleasures wait,

No room adorned with pomp and pride of state,
No richly-coloured window opes to sight
Bright prospects of magnificent delight,
No gilded canopy o'erhung his head,
Nor costliest coverings o'er his couch lay spread ;
But better still, no spectres of affright
Palsied his heart, and terrified his sight ;
No lingering tortures racked his aching bones,
Nor from his bosom wrung the bursting groans.
One form there stood, adorned with gentle grace,
And met his glance with loving, smiling face,
Her silvery voice invited him to share
The ready feast of savoury wholesome fare.
Again the boon was given for which he yearned—
His home, his wife, his comforts had returned.
Awaked, he found the past a hideous dream,
And grateful tears of sweet contentment stream
He blessed the vision that had freed his heart
From the envenomed power of MAMMON's dart.
Once more with cheerful steps he gladly trod
Life's round of duty in the fear of God.

BIRTHDAY WISHES.

EQUESTED as a friend
  To celebrate in verse thy natal day,
    Sincerity may lend
  Some value to an unpretending lay.

    And what boon unpossessed
Shall friendship wish for thee, not yet bestowed ?
    Already richly blessed
By the kind mercy of thy loving God.

    I dare not wish thee wealth—
Seldom is happiness with gold combined ;
    But competence and health,
May these be thine with a contented mind.

    I do not wish thee free
From the temptations and the snares of life—
    I know this cannot be ;
I wish thee strength and victory in the strife.

I wish thee not earth's fame,
Which, whilst it crowns the brow, oft stabs the heart ;
But mayst thou ever claim
With heaven's nobility thy better part.

I wish that thou mayst shine
With borrowed heavenly beams, serenely bright,
And by thy rays divine
Guide many a wanderer to the plains of light.

One purpose mayst thou know,
And may it rule and govern all thy days,
To live and die below,
To glorify the power of saving grace.

And when earth's fondest ties
By distance or by death's cold hand are riven,
May faith anoint thine eyes
To see th' unsinning meeting place in heaven.

And when is heard at length
Thy call to join the disembodied throng,
Then, in thy Saviour's strength
O'ercoming, mayst thou swell the victors' song.

TO MY FATHER.

GAIN my willing heart and hand shall pay
　　A tribute to thy worth ;
And wake the muse in honour of the day
　　That gave my father birth.

My childhood's friend, and guide of giddy youth,
　　The precepts thou hast given
Have sought to win to paths of peace and truth,
　　And train thy child for heaven.

And fear not that thy tender watchful care
　　Shall ever be forgot ;
My grateful heart shall still thine image bear
　　With holiest memories fraught.

Chequered, my father, hath thy life-path been,
　　Alternate light and shade ;
And it hath led through many a changing scene,
　　Hill, forest, streamlet, glade.

But up each steep ascent thy Saviour's hand
    Thy faltering steps hath led ;
And beams of glory from the better land
    Have pierced through Sorrow's shade.

And now thy foot grows weary, and thy brow
    Is crowned with silvery white ;
And oft perchance to Faith's keen vision now
    The goal appears in sight.

Brighter and brighter may a light divine
    Illumine nature's gloom ;
May God's unclouded smile upon thee shine,
    Maturing thee for home.

But earnestly and hopefully I pray,
    If such God's holy will,
Thou yet through many a coming natal day
    Mayst tarry with us still.

And when Time's hand hath laid us one by one
    To death's long quiet rest,
May we be found united round the throne
    For ever safe and blest.

CHRISTMAS.

WE twine our Christmas wreaths,
    And we scatter our Christmas flowers,
And our gay bright garlands rival
    The summer's rosy bowers.
    And the air no longer vocal
With the music of the bird,
Now 'midst the winter's stillness
    By the Christmas song is stirred.

We spread the Christmas feast,
    And we gather our loved ones round ;
And we mark Time's stealthy traces
    On the altering features sound.
For the young are growing older,
    And the old are waning fast,
And perchance some place is vacant
    Since we assembled last.

We pile the Christmas fire
    Till it blazes warm and bright ;

And eye meets eye with glances
    Enkindled with love's pure light.
And the storms of care and sorrow
    For a brief, glad season stilled,
With affection's holiest feelings
    Our softening hearts are filled.

Let us breathe the Christmas spirit,
    Peace and good-will to all ;
Let charity warm our bosoms,
    And accents of kindness fall.
And attuned to love's sweet key-note,
    Let our hearts and voices sing
Of Heaven's matchless, richest blessing—
    The birth of our Saviour King.

A HAPPY NEW YEAR.

 HAPPY New Year! how the glad countless
        voices
    Re-echo the old well-known words to and
        fro!
    Whilst each heart with a feeling of fresh-
        ness rejoices,
And affection's pure, holiest gushings outflow.

A happy New Year! and the bright young eye glistens
    With rose-tinted visions of coming delight;—
A happy New Year! and the aged ear listens,
    And smiles light the darkness of gathering night.

The past hath been pregnant with wondrous unfolding
    Of world-startling changes in many a land;
And the hope-gilded promise the future is holding
    Of scenes far more bright, and achievements more
        grand.

For the thrones of the despots, and systems of error,
  Are trembling, and tottering, and doomed to decay;
And Truth hath arisen, in glory and terror,
  To chase Superstition's dark curtains away.

And Knowledge and Science their torches are lighting
  Where thickest the clouds of dark ignorance roll;
And the poor dazzled, startled ones, now are inviting
  To the banquet of reason—the feast of the soul.

And the dark reign of Guilt, the foul monster, is ending,
  Though mighty its last dying struggles and throes;
For the sway of the Saviour is sweetly extending,
  And salvation's bright stream ever widening flows.

Then with hope all around us, and heaven above us;
  With voices and hearts full of courage and cheer;
We will greet, as we meet, all the dear ones who love us,
  With the old heartfelt accents, "A happy New Year."

TO A BRIDE.

AY He who honoured Cana's feast
    With presence and with power,
Vouchsafe, as an approving guest,
    To bless thy bridal hour.

May angel hands entwine a wreath,
    Of flow'rets rare and blest ;
Love, Hope, Joy, Constancy, and Faith,
    Upon thy brow to rest.

Brighter than Sol's inspiring dart
    On eastern pinion borne,
May cloudless sunshine of the heart
    Illume thy bridal morn.

May prayers from many a faithful friend
    Like wafted odours rise,
And answering heavenly gifts descend
    From Him who rules the skies.

May duties new bring new delight
    Increasing day by day ;
May hearts and souls with hands unite
    To smooth life's rugged way.

New wisdom, with new cares be given,
    And cheer'd by love divine ;
May earthly bliss and hopes of heaven,
    Encircle thee and thine.

And when to heaven's eternal feast
    The trumpet-call shall sound,
With well-trimmed lamp, and spotless dress,
    Mayst thou be ready found.

"UNTO HIM EVERY KNEE SHALL BOW."

YES! unto Him, the cradled babe of Bethle-
  hem's lowly manger,
 Where the astonished shepherds ran to
  greet the wondrous stranger—
 The Lord of life, the Source of light, the
  Fountain of creation,
God !—born as man, as man to die, for fallen man's
 salvation.

Yes ! unto Him, the homeless One, His followers meekly
 telling,
Foxes have holes, and birds have nests, I have no earthly
 dwelling.
Behold Him, not in pomp and state, but poor, despised,
 rejected,
Yet the one true Messiah He—long promised, long
 expected.

Yes ! unto Him, the stricken One, in the lone garden
 bending,

Whilst from His body, crushed with grief, the blood-
    sweat is descending,
Anon, by cruel ruffian bands of mocking soldiers taken,
And by His own beloved ones, in that dark hour forsaken.

Yes ! unto Him, outstretched on yonder cross to bleed
    and languish,
Enduring more than mortal pain—greater than earthly
    anguish ;
The weight that would have crushed a world upon His
    soul is lying,
Whilst rending rocks and quaking earth proclaim their
    Maker dying.

Yes ! unto Him, the risen One, the grave's dark fetters
    spurning,
And from the vanquished realm of death victoriously
    returning.
Alone He waged the dreadful fight in garments red and
    gory,
Alone He triumphs in His might, and reigns the King
    of glory.

Yes ! unto Him, upon His head, the "many crowns"
    now wearing,
Yet, in His exaltation, still our name and nature bearing ;
The highest ranks of angel hosts, in wonder lowly bending,
Search, and still find love's mysteries far beyond their
    comprehending.

And lo ! the ransomed bow the knee from every clime
    and nation,
The black and white, the bond and free, all kneel in
    adoration ;
The lisping infant clasps the hands, and reverently and
    slowly,
Learns from the lips of riper age to render homage lowly.

The monarch lays aside his crown, and earthly rank
    concealing,
Now at a mightier monarch's throne, is, like the peasant,
    kneeling ;
The honoured sons of world-wide fame, away their laurels
    flinging,
Are crowding to the Saviour's feet, love's grateful incense
    bringing.

And e'en the maddened multitude, who, in their wild,
    blind error,
Reject and slight Him, they shall see Him robed in
    dreadful terror ;
They too shall fall before His throne, in anguish un-
    availing,
And hear the dreadful word " Depart ! " with hopeless,
    bitter wailing.

E'en thus, Redeemer, triumph, till Thy mighty work is
    ended,

Till the last of Thy redeemed ones to Thy presence hath
  ascended ;
Till a new earth and heaven shall ceaseless hymns of
  praise be pouring,
And countless saints cast countless crowns, before Thy
  feet adoring.

WHY CANNOT WE ALL LIVE AS BRETHREN?

WHY cannot we all live as brethren
 In this beautiful world here below?
Why should envy, or hatred, or discord,
 Enhance the dark tale of our woe?

Where our smile, or our word, or our blessing,
 Might a sun-ray of comfort impart;
Why should selfishness with her cold finger
 Freeze up the warm springs of the heart?

Have we mounted some steps in life's ladder,
 And heaped a few grains of bright dust?
Ne'er be holy affection's pearls slighted
 In riches uncertain to trust!

Are others a trifle above us?
 Then let us ne'er envy their state;
If we can, let us win them to love us,
 If not,—be *our* minds free from hate.

Has our neighbour his faults or his failings?
    Ah! surely he stands not alone!
When we sit down to judge and condemn them,
    Let us honestly bring forth our own.

Has the hand that should rather have blessed us
    Dealt out to our bosoms a wound?
It may be in error of judgment,
    Excuse for the act can be found.

Have the eyes that once sparkled with kindness,
    Proud, heart-chilling, cold glances thrown?
Stay! judge not too harshly,—those glances
    Perchance but reflected thine own.

Hath a dark blow been aimed without mercy
    At thy character, prospects, or heart?
Resentment is *man's* pride and glory—
    Forgiveness is God's nobler part.

Wouldst thou bind minds, as varied as faces,
    In one creed, or one party, or name?
Nay! gracefully yield to another
    The freedom of thought *thou* wouldst claim.

When—when shall the bright peaceful morning
    O'er our war-blighted world its light shed?
When the apple of discord no longer
    Its bliss-blighting influence shall spread.

When—when shall Earth's scenes of commotion,
    Of envies and jealousies cease ?
And the roar of the waves of contention
    Be hushed to the stillness of Peace ?

Then !—then !—when men wiser and warier
    Shall fathom the cause of their woe,
And see the arch Tempter delighting
    The seeds of dissension to sow.

Then !—then !—when the love of Immanuel
    Universally governs each soul,
Then our earth shall be one happy brotherhood,
    And Concord and Peace bind the whole.

TO APRIL.

STILL true to thy character, smiling and frown-
ing,
Fickle April, once more thou art come.
Now Heaven's bright sunbeams thy cloud-
less brow crowning,
Now enveloped in darkness and gloom.

Now, from thy blue sky such bright glory is peeping,
We deem that it cannot but last ;
A moment, and dark clouds are over it sweeping,
And the heart-cheering vision is past.

Yet though thy dark, changeful moods still are deceiving
The hopes to which sunshine gives birth,
Still, April, we love thee : we know thou art weaving
A beautiful mantle for earth.

Thou art waking with sunshine, and softening with
showers
The slumbering frost-hardened ground ;
Unlocking the storehouse of blossoms and flowers,
And scattering fresh life-seeds around.

And for each teeming shower that thy rich clouds are
    bearing,
  The future more brilliant shall be ;
And for each gloomy frown that thy dark brow is wear-
    ing
  Brighter smiles the glad summer shall see.

E'en thus, changing April, our life sky above us
  Is varied with sunshine and gloom;
Now brightened and cheered by the dear ones that
    love us,
  Now raining sad tears o'er the tomb.

Now mirth-lighted moments and beamings of gladness
  Shed transport too pure here to last ;
Now a dark cloud of grief and heart-withering sadness,
  O'er the beautiful prospect is cast.

But as April is needful to aid the unfolding
  Of summer's bright verdure and bloom,
So e'en sorrows and troubles our spirits are moulding
  For the bliss of our heavenly home.

Let us bravely look onward, nor ever surrender
  Our faith in the care of our God ;
His Providence, watchful, and gracious, and tender,
  Overrules every change for our good.

TO SPRING.

COME ! lovely spring-tide come !
    We have waited for thee long :
    For stern winter seemed to linger,
    And with cold and icy finger
    Bound the earth in fetters strong :
We wait thy breath to warm,
We wait thy power to charm
Into beauty, life, and song,
Awakening Nature rising from her dark and wintry tomb

    Come, with the bird and flower !
    With the blossom for the tree !
    And ten thousand smiles shall meet thee,
    And ten thousand hearts shall greet thee,
    As thou flingest wide and free
        Sunshine, and bud, and bloom,
        Life, fragrance, and perfume ;
        And our hearts yield peacefully
To the holy, soothing influence of thy sweet, resistless
    power.

Come ! dry our weeping eyes !
We have mourned 'neath winter's gloom ;
We have seen our hopes decaying,
And in sorrow have been laying
Faded loved ones in the tomb.
Come ! bid our faith look up,
As thou breathest holy hope,
That Eternal Spring shall come,
Scattering death's dark wintry shadows, with the sun-
shine of the skies.

JOHN HEYWOOD, PRINTER, MANCHESTER.